"What are you trying to pull, Charlie? . . .

Aren't you a little old to interfere in your father's life?" Cort's low-pitched voice was dangerously soft.

Charlie stiffened at his implication, repeated now for the second time since her arrival. Evidently she had two strikes against her.

Cort must think she had purposely resigned from the LPGA to follow her father to Mexico and discourage his interest in beginning a new, independent career; and now, sensing Jim Summers' possible interest in his sister Marita, was attempting to warn him against such an alliance before it was launched. She was innocent of both charges! The urge to fight back ballooned.

"I'm waiting." She could hear the harsh rhythm of his breathing mere inches above her ear.

"You'll have to wait a long time, Cort," she mumbled mutinously. "Golf is the only game I play." Her pulse fluttered alarmingly in her throat, but she didn't budge.

"Who said we were playing a game?"

HALFWAY TO HEAVEN

Nancy Olander Johanson

Serenade/Serenata
BOOKS
of the Zondervan Publishing House
Grand Rapids, Michigan

HALFWAY TO HEAVEN
Copyright © 1985 by Nancy O. Johanson

Serenade/Serenata is an imprint of
The Zondervan Publishing House
1415 Lake Drive, S.E.
Grand Rapids, MI 49506

ISBN 0-310-46752-7

Edited by Anne Severance
Designed by Kim Koning

Printed in the United States of America

85 86 87 88 89 90 / 10 9 8 7 6 5 4 3 2 1

For Kirstin, with love
Romans Twelve

CHAPTER 1

"YOU'RE GOING TO WHAT! If this is your idea of a joke, Charlie, I'm not finding it a bit humorous. You're out of your mind. I won't permit it!"

Charline Summers glanced hurriedly around the crowded dining room of the country club before glaring across the table at her father.

"I knew you'd say that, Dad, but you might as well save your arguments. I've given this decision considerable thought, and I refuse to be cajoled into changing my mind."

Her father lowered his voice one decibel and glared back. "If this outburst is a result of your thought processes these days, you're either in need of a psychiatrist or that spanking I always threatened and never delivered."

Fidgeting with the bows of sunglasses snatched from the crown of her sun-bleached honey-blond hair, Charlie congratulated herself for purposely choosing this particular time and place to inform Jim Summers of her intention to take a year's hiatus from the pro golf circuit.

She and her father were sharing lunch and discussing her spectacular win at the Mayflower Classic in Indianapolis, only the day before. Lunch at the Palm Springs club, where her father was golf pro and manager, was an intimate custom dating from her first tournament win as a professional golfer at the age of eighteen. It had been repeated several times a year for eight years, always here where she had been patiently instructed in the sport by a bereaved father suffering the cruel loss of his beautiful wife and only son, killed in a tragic car accident. He had not known what to do with a young daughter, and a series of housekeepers had failed to meet their mutual needs.

Charlie smiled at Jim's reference to spankings. He had spoiled her rotten, and she had repaid him by doing everything in her power to make him proud of her. Fortunately her father had recognized her athletic talent and had encouraged her to try golf. Because of his work at the club, she had taken advantage of the endless opportunities to watch men and women, professionals and amateurs, in action. Several famous personalities had been her constant inspiration.

Charlie had played through the usual rounds of children's amateur tournaments, and then joined the high school varsity teams. Jim hadn't objected when she dropped out of college to turn pro after completing only one year. She had amassed every amateur title available, including the United States Juniors title at age seventeen, so it had been a natural step. Her father had not hidden his pleasure with her decision to make golf her career.

"I know this comes as a shock to you, Dad." Charlie looked anxiously at Jim across the table for two. "There was no easy way to tell you; but if you will listen to my reasons for taking a hiatus, I know you'll agree they're good ones."

"Never. I can't think of a single motive, outside of a permanent disability, to make the top woman golfer in the country throw in the towel. My stars, Charlie! You've won five tournaments this year, including both the United States Open and the Ladies' Professional Golf Association title. You're riding the crest of a winning streak, the envy of every woman golfer in the world, not to mention a few men. *You can't quit! Golf is your life!*"

"Terrific. Don't you see, Dad . . . that's the whole problem."

"Problem! There's not a woman in this room who wouldn't exchange what she's got for your so-called problem," Jim argued. "Your name is a household word. You're adored by the public, and sought after by the press, the movie and television industries. You're independently wealthy, able to buy anything your heart desires. You're living the American Dream, Charlie."

Smiling briefly at his choice of words, Charlie nodded acquiescence. "I'm living in the limelight, all right, Dad. In a way, it's exciting and glamorous and rewarding . . . I can't deny that." She paused, refolding her napkin into a perfect square. "And, in a way, I have needed the attention my tenuous fame has provided, but it isn't enough anymore. Not every dream is worth pursuing . . . not if it becomes a nightmare." Her voice lowered significantly. "Being in the winner's circle isn't everything."

"I can't believe what I'm hearing. You're young, healthy, and beautiful. You've got the world at your feet. You can make your dreams anything you want them to be."

"Stop it, Dad! You're not hearing what I'm saying. You, of all people, don't believe what you're saying to me, either!"

Jim was immediately contrite. Motioning to the waiter, he hastily signed their luncheon bill, took Charlie by the elbow and steered her through the room, completely oblivious to the greetings of club regulars watching their exit.

"Come on, honey. I know now why you chose this three-ring circus for your announcement, but it's no place to talk. We'll go home. And don't worry, there won't be any more temper tantrums from your old man. I might be bullheaded at times, but I got your message loud and clear."

It was a silent trip. With each mile, Charlie fought her guilty conscience. Since her mother's death, her professional career had kept Jim Summers going month after month, year after year, while waiting for the healing of his grief. Between tournaments, he had spent endless hours in practice sessions with her, teaching her everything he knew about golf, and then more hours in discussions at home afterward. He had traveled the country with her in pursuit of the dream to which he had alluded at the club. Their mutual interest in golf had kept them close, and given them a purpose for continuing their lives as a family of only two. Now it must seem to him that she was the most ungrateful daughter in the world.

Watching Jim as he concentrated on his driving, Charlie wondered if devoting so much of his life to her career had been worth all the sacrifices he must have made. Time had been kind to him, though. At forty-seven, the dusting of white in his sideburns, and throughout the sandy-brown hair curling in thick waves around his permanently tanned face, only added to his physical attractiveness and virility. He must have caught the attention of a long string of single women. How insensitive she had been not to be aware of that before now. He should have remarried and enjoyed a second family . . . another son, perhaps.

Turning to look out the car window, Charlie brushed a hand over her eyes. It wasn't too late. She had to be strong for his sake, as well as for her own. It was time for them to go their separate ways.

"Well, honey girl, are we going to go in?"

Charlie gave a start when she realized they were parked in the driveway in front of their house. She smiled reassuringly. "Of course, Dad. I was just thinking how good coming home feels after being on the road."

Jim studied the small brick dwelling nestled amidst the full grown palms and cacti which characterized a typical Palm Springs desert landscape. "I'm glad you feel that way. Somehow, I could never make myself sell this place and move. This was the first house your mother and I bought . . . the only one, as it turned out." He patted Charlie's hand lying on the car seat between them. "Old habits die hard. This little place has been okay for the two of us, though, hasn't it?"

Charlie swallowed the strange lump in her throat and nodded. "Sure has," she said quickly, leaning sideways in a spontaneous gesture to drop a kiss onto his cheek. Jerking the door handle down, she pushed herself out onto the paved driveway and paused to take a deep, ragged sigh. Leaving was going to be harder than she thought.

"Come on, gal, quit your dawdling."

"Who's dawdling? I'm catching my breath after stuffing myself on that fantastic meal you arranged."

Jim Summers laughed and held out his hand for hers. Together, they walked up the sidewalk to the front door of the three-bedroom cottage. "Like I said, old habits . . ."

" . . . die hard," Charlie conceded, giving his arm a squeeze.

Upon entering the house, she thought how cold and impersonal it felt, as sparsely furnished as any one of the motel rooms she had occupied from coast to coast. Nothing had been added since the early days of her parents' marriage, when household needs took second place to those of two growing children. There had been no need to make changes, though. She and her father seldom entertained, and on those few occasions, it seemed more convenient to use the club.

"Let's go into the study, Charlie. Can I get you anything? Some coffee?"

"Nothing for me, Dad, but I'll be glad to get some for you." She stalled, looking for any excuse to put off the discussion causing the awkwardness between them.

"I'm fine."

He took off the crisp navy linen blazer worn over a white golf shirt, and threw it over the back of an armchair in one corner of the crowded study. Running his fingers through his hair, he paused to look around the small room crammed with trophies and mementos. "Look at this place. Where are we going to find room to put yesterday's trophy? There isn't enough room to turn around in here."

"It doesn't matter, Dad."

"Of course, it does. We should sell this place and get a bigger one. Why don't we build something? We should have a suitable study for you—one with a business office, and we should have a separate trophy room. I've thought of it several times, but we've always been too busy to do anything about it."

"Dad . . ."

Jim turned, his hands on his hips, a concerned look on his face. "Okay, Charline, out with it. What's this business about wanting to quit the pro circuit?"

"Ouch." Charlie grimaced and playfully tossed a pencil at him. "You haven't called me Charline for years, not since I lost the St. Petersburg Open by one stroke. I missed a two-foot putt on the 18th hole. Remember?"

"I remember. You thought it was an easy shot and tried to tap the ball in with some fancy one-handed swing. That ball went sailing across the green like it had wings."

"You waited until I had waded through the astonished gallery before admonishing me. 'Charline,' you said in a very stern voice, 'a winner refuses to take even *one inch* for granted!' "

Sharing the pleasant memory broke the ice, and, chuckling in relaxed companionship, they settled on a worn tweed couch. Jim curled an arm around Charline's shoulders, and she nestled her head against his side, propping her long coltish legs on top of the low magazine table in front of them. She could hear the slow, steady beating of her father's heart, and somehow she drew strength and courage from its sound. In this favorite position, she felt safe, secure.

"This is more like it, honey girl. We've always been able to talk in this room, haven't we? Start from the beginning now. Why have you made such a momentous decision?"

The huskiness in his voice got to her, and she pressed her lips together to steady the quiver in her chin before answering. "I'm tired, Dad." Her voice faltered and the ensuing silence stretched interminably.

"I see. That's it? You're physically tired?"

"Physically, and mentally too," she continued hurriedly. "We haven't stopped for one minute, you know—not once in eight years. The pressure and the constant travel have been very fatiguing. The press doesn't let up, and the tournament directors expect so much more of me now. They say the galleries aren't as large if I don't participate in every tournament. Lately the cold weather, the wet fairways, the wind, the sand in my face from those hateful traps, the incessant sunburns . . . they're all beginning to get to me. I'm tired of hunting for laundromats, of sleeping in strange beds, and of packing my suitcase one more time."

When she stopped speaking, the echo of her words sounded petty and childish. Her father was too intelligent to accept such an inane explanation. A professional golfer . . . any pro . . . learned to accept such things as part of the inevitable reality of working toward a successful career.

"There are no real challenges left for me in golf, Dad. I've won all the major tournaments, many of them more than once. I've been on the road for eight years as a professional, and it's not fun any more." Charlie paused to take another lengthy sigh. "I've prayed long and hard about this decision, Dad. That might come as a surprise to you, too. There haven't been many opportunities for me to attend church services while on the road, and I know you've been concerned. Since weekends are always used for tournaments, I haven't been as close to the Lord as I used to be. I need some time to put various things in my life back into the proper perspective."

Her father's hand affectionately rumpled the silken curls spilled out across his shoulder. "Are you regretting your broken engagement to Dean Connally, honey? Is that what this is really about?"

Charlie sat up with a jerk. "Of course not!" she denied, catching herself just in time to stay calm. "That was finished and done with months ago. You know that!"

"I know that's what you said, but I could see you were hurting at the time. I thought you might have changed your mind."

"Well, I haven't. I felt a little sad and regretful at the time— rejection isn't pleasant—but, Dean was more perceptive than I. He wants a wife, a home, and kids. I'm always on the road. It wouldn't have worked for us. Anyway, after the initial trauma subsided, I realized I didn't really love him, not in the special way you and Mom loved each other."

"Are you certain, Charlie? I have a feeling Dean still loves you, if my interpretation of his recent inquiries is correct."

Charlie left the couch and her father's probing eyes, and walked to the sliding glass door opening onto a small patio outside the study. She started to push it aside and then remembered the air conditioning was on.

Had her father noticed how his words had rattled her? She could never confide to him the details of the evening Dean asked for the return of his ring. The working relationship between the two men would be destroyed. Her doting father would find it impossible to forgive Dean for causing her such bitter unhappiness.

The day after winning the Dinah Shore Tournament several months ago, Charlie had rushed home to accompany Dean Connally to the annual charity ball held at the club. It was the most important function of the year for him, a showcase for his expertise and talent as the manager of the nationally famous private golf facility in Palm Springs.

Dean had spent months in preparation for the event, and the promise that former President Gerald Ford and entertainer Bob Hope would attend assured Dean's recognition from guests and the media, and even more importantly, from Charlie herself.

She had failed him miserably. From the very beginning of the evening, she had made one *faux pas* after another.

The day had begun exactly like this one. Because of her father's inability to forgo traditions, they had celebrated her tournament win with a much too extravagant meal at the club. The rich food, combined with her physical fatigue and the emotional letdown that always followed the end of a tournament, proved a lethal combination. Returning home—with every intention of spending the afternoon repairing the ravages of too much sun, wind, and grit to her skin and hair—she had, instead, fallen soundly asleep on her bed.

Dean had arrived at six-thirty, eager to see her and to squire a proud and radiant fiancée to the gala. Finding her still in dreamland, her father had given Dean the deflating news as gently as possible. Fuming and frustrated, Dean had gone on alone, with only assurances that she would join him as soon as possible.

She did her best to hurry, but an hour-and-a-half wait and two or more drinks did nothing to restore Dean's good humor. She had worked feverishly to make it up to him, laughing at all his jokes, throwing him adoring looks, clinging to his arm with obvious, almost dripping, devotion. She loved him. She had wanted to prove it.

Somehow she had failed to notice his frowning disapproval of her uncommonly public display, or to listen to his feeble attempts to laugh it off in front of their friends.

Later, she had carelessly passed off his embarrassment when, while he was speaking with reporters, she had accidentally spilled a glass of red punch on him, staining the pants of his tuxedo in ugly spots. She had dismissed his barely concealed anger when she yawned audibly during his televised speech of welcome to the elite guests, outlining the benefits provided to the community by their financial support of the spectacular charity event. In retrospect, she could now accept the results of her insensitive performance, but for months, she had blamed Dean completely for their break-up.

The evening in shambles, Dean had suggested they leave as soon as his formal duties were completed. She had appreciated his understanding of her fatigue. When he followed her into the house, she had urged him to go back to the party.

"I'm sorry I'm such poor company tonight, Dean, but there's no reason you should miss any more of the evening. I love you darling, and I'm terribly proud of you." She had smiled and reached up to give him a gentle kiss.

"Prove it, Charlie. You've been driving me crazy tonight." Dean had pulled her into his arms with uncharacteristic roughness, kissing her with more passion than he had ever exhibited.

16

"Oh, Charlie, Charlie," he moaned, raining her face with a quick succession of little kisses. "Let me make love to you tonight. I can't wait any longer, darling. I'm going insane with all this waiting."

Pressing against his chest with her hands, she had succeeded in putting more space between them. "Not tonight, Dean. Not this way. We . . . we need to make such a momentous event more special . . . a-and you know I don't feel right about compromising my Christian beliefs."

"You're not being fair, Charlie," Dean had complained. "You led me on all evening with your public billing and cooing, and now you want me to turn it off with the snap of a finger. I go out of my mind waiting for you to come home from tournaments, and when you get here, you lead me on, only to push me away. I can't keep it up!" He had pulled her close once more, and kissed her with mounting passion, his lips grinding against hers. Pinioned in his arms, it was difficult to move. Finally she had twisted her head aside with great effort.

"Dean, please! My father might come home."

Dean had dragged his fingers through his red-blond hair, and down over his face, dismissing her pitiful protests. "Your *father!* That's another thing. You're too old to be living with him. Isn't it about time you got a place of your own . . . one with some privacy? You're not a juvenile needing the protection of her daddy."

She had schooled her voice to respond with patience. "You're simply not behaving like your usual self tonight, Dean. I didn't purposely lead you on tonight, and I didn't intentionally try to humiliate you, either. I'm tired, and my attempts to show you how much I care for you were evidently bungled because of it." Her voice had caught on a sob, and frighteningly close to tears, she had rushed on. "'I'm sorry honey I really am, but my loving you, and your

17

loving me, doesn't mean I owe you sex just because you want it. I don't *owe* you anything. Love isn't taking what you want from a person, when you want it. To me, love is accepting what is offered, and giving what is needed at that moment of time. Love is patience and understanding."

"Love is also knowing when a man needs more than sisterly kisses and . . . teasing! Love knows when patience has come to an end, and mine has, Charlie! In case you haven't noticed, I'm a man, not a high school kid. If you don't want to marry me yet, at least we can live together in an apartment of our own when you're here between tournaments. Don't you care about my happiness at all?"

"Of *course* I do, Dean!" she had insisted lamely while wondering if their conversation was really a bad dream. Her Christian life might have been inactive at the time, but she had always respected basic Christian beliefs. "Maybe I have taken your love for granted sometimes, and kept you waiting longer than you'd like," she had conceded, "but we wouldn't have much of a marriage with me on the road most of the time. Besides, if sex is all you want from me, then maybe you don't love me after all."

"Maybe you don't love *me* ! Have you ever thought of that? Don't you think, at age twenty-six, you should be interested in more than kisses? Enough of this. It's time for you to make a decision, Charlie. Do we get married, or not?"

"Not yet. I can't." Even after all that, she had resorted to stalling rather than making a decision. "I have two more tournaments coming up, an interview with *Golf Digest,* and a series of commercials for the line of sportswear carrying my name. You already know my schedule. Please, Dean, don't make demands on me now. Be patient awhile longer. A few more months and we'll set a date. I promise."

Dean had refused. "I've had enough. I want a

woman who cares more about me than about having her name and face plastered from one end of the world to the other; someone who isn't afraid to leave her daddy's hip pocket; who will allow him to live his own life while she lives hers. We're through, Charlie. As of now, you owe me nothing—not that you've ever given me much in the past. I don't think you're even capable of loving a man . . . except for your precious daddy, of course!''

''You don't mean this, Dean. You're angry about tonight.'' She understood his need to lash out at her, but angry words could kill a relationship, and his had deeply wounded her already. ''Can't we meet in the morning and talk about it when we're both rested?'' She had actually stood there and pleaded, humiliating herself in the process.

''There's nothing more to say.''

''Do you . . . do you want your ring back?'' She had fingered the large brilliant diamond hesitantly, uncertainly.

Dean had paused at the door to look back at her. For a fleeting instant she had seen a glimmer of regret in his eyes, and then, steeling himself, he had stalked over to her and held out his hand.

''Sure. Why not? You can afford to buy yourself another more easily than I can. I'll use it for your replacement.''

With an angry gesture, she had torn the ring off her finger and shoved it into his open palm, turning to run down the hall to her room before he could slam the front door in her presence.

She had made no more than a two-sentence explanation to her father the next morning. ''Dean asked for his ring back last night. I agreed with him that we're not ready for marriage.''

Although she had never discussed it again, Dean's words became a persistently festering boil. Was she able to love a man other than her father? She needed to find out. Was she responsible for keeping Jim from living a private life? She would make sure he had his freedom.

"I'm sorry for bringing up Dean's name, honey girl," Jim was saying now. "I never thought the two of you were suited for each other, but I want you to be happy. I'm glad you aren't pining for him." When she didn't immediately respond, he continued, "I owe you an apology for attempting to push you into decisions that aren't in your best interests. I should have been the first one to counsel you about letting God have His way in your life. He has given you an incredible talent, Charlie, but He wants you to use it for His glory, not your own. If withdrawing from the tournament circuit for a year or so is what you feel God wants for you, then I won't stand in your way. I'll continue to pray for your happiness and for the Lord's guidance in your future plans."

"Thanks, Dad. I knew I could count on you." At last assured of her father's support, Charlie felt her confidence return, and she faced him once more with a grin. "I confess I thought I'd have to argue the issue for days, not minutes!"

Jim Summers joined her laughter. "Surprised you, did I? It must be a sign of old age. I'm getting soft."

"If you're fishing for another compliment, I'll give it only one more time. You're not old; you're in your prime. What you need, my dear father, is to get away from this place for a while, and find yourself some adoring female companion to feed that ego of yours on a full-time basis."

"You mean . . . get married again?"

"Sure. Why not?"

"You wouldn't mind?"

Charlie heard the amazement in her father's voice and attempted to keep hers light. Could Dean have been right? "Of course not. Do you have someone in mind?"

"No, not really. I just always thought . . ." He broke off abruptly, waving away the reply with a gesture. "Let's talk about *you*, not me. Have you given any thought to what you'll do when you withdraw from the circuit?"

"Not entirely, but I firmly believe God will direct me. That's to be part of my hiatus . . . to get back into sync with my Maker. I thought I'd take a few months to relax. I need to unwind, without the pressures of the press and the tournament directors breathing down my neck."

"That's going to be rather hard to do if you stick around here . . . but I have a suggestion, if you'd care to hear it."

"Sure. Suggest away. I'm all ears."

Jim gave her a troubled look, pausing to bite on a lip before leaning forward in a thoughtful attitude. Clasping and unclasping his hands, he confessed, "I've accepted a job designing a championship golf facility for an old buddy of mine in Manzanillo, Mexico. I was planning to tell you, and then you threw me your own surprise tonight. It's not a permanent move. I'll only be taking a year's leave, like you. I've always wanted to be the architect of an extraordinary golf course. Actually, Cort has enticed me before this for other courses he needed, but I never felt I could take the time necessary to do a good job."

He paused again, and threw her a glance. "You're not mad, are you, Charlie? I didn't want to say anything until I had decided for sure to take the offer."

"Of course I'm not mad. I'm thrilled for you. I'm rather surprised, that's all. I've never heard you mention wanting to design golf courses before." Her voice thickened and she blinked to keep back the swiftly forming tears. "Oh, Dad, it's my fault you haven't been able to take such grand offers before this, isn't it? I've been so . . . selfish." Her head dropped against her knees, and she felt her shoulder-length hair fall forward around her face, hiding her shame.

Jim was beside her in a second, lifting her face and dabbing at the wet smears on her cheeks with a clean andkerchief. "I refuse to accept pity from anyone, ınd most especially from you, Charline. You have not oeen selfish, and I have not sacrificed anything because of you. Until now, I haven't been ready to make a change in my career."

"But, all those other offers . . ."

"I wasn't interested when they were made. I didn't feel competent enough for the undertaking. Now, I do. Understand?"

Charlie sniffed and pulled the rumpled hanky from his hand, scrubbing vigorously to dry her still blurring eyes. "Uh-huh. I guess so. When do you go?"

"Cort suggested the first of the month, and I have permission to leave my job here at that time. Dean has already hired an assistant to take over in my absence."

"I see." Charlie smiled weakly. "You have it all worked out. That doesn't leave us much time to get you packed. About a week and a half. I'll . . . miss you."

"That's what I wanted to talk about, honey. Why don't you come with me? Cort's place is a perfect hideaway for you. It's fairly isolated, on the west coast of Mexico, and the press isn't likely to follow you there."

"Thanks for wanting me with you, Dad, but I don't think it would be a good idea. In the first place, I'm sure your friend doesn't expect you to have a grown daughter in tow; and, in the second place, I really need to work out my future on my own. I've leaned too heavily on you up to now. You need to live your life without me in your hip pocket." Unconsciously, she used Dean's words. They had been on her mind for too many weeks.

"Nonsense. You're my daughter, and always will be. I can't stop caring at the snap of a finger. And Cort will be delighted to have you along. We'll stay at his home, not in the hotel."

"All the more reason why I shouldn't go along. I'm positive his wife would have fits. No woman likes unexpected house guests."

"Cort isn't married. He used to be, but Helena died several years ago of cancer."

"How tragic."

"Yes. Especially so, because of her youth." Jim's similar personal loss was evident in his voice, but Charlie chose to ignore it.

"Your friend is your age, then?"

"He's several years younger, around thirty-five, I think. I met him here at the club. You met him once, but may not remember. He was a spectacular rising star of the men's Professional Golf Association. At that time, he was the only Mexican-American on the pro tour, and a Californian of considerable fame. That combination, along with his remarkable skill, made him a favorite with the press and the fans. He could have been as famous as Lee Trevino, if he hadn't quit golf altogether."

"Now I *am* curious. What's his last name, and why did he quit?"

"His full name is Cortez Ruillon, and it's rumored he quit playing when his wife died, either out of grief over her death, or guilt because he wasn't with her when it happened. Others say he would have returned, if his brother-in-law hadn't been killed in a plane crash, leaving Cort's only sister alone with a young son to raise. He took them into his home and concentrated on investing his golf winnings in resort properties around the world. He's built up quite an impressive empire."

"Sounds like *quite* a guy. No wonder you want to do business with him."

"You can meet him . . . if you come with me, Charlie."

"Thanks, but no thanks. I'll stay home." She hopped off the desk and moved toward the door of the study. "When do you think I should make my announcement public, Dad?"

"I'll call a press conference for Friday afternoon. That will give us four days to notify the LPGA directors of your decision, and to write up an official statement. We need to check with your agent on any legalities involved, and make certain we don't permanently shut doors that we might want reopened later. How does that sound to you?"

"Fine. You know what's best in that department." She carefully examined the toe of one slightly scuffed shoe. "I'm grateful for your help and support, Dad, but I can handle most of the actual work myself, and Donn can take care of the rest. You'll have enough to do getting your own things in order."

"We'll work together on both, as we've always done, Charlie."

The next four days passed in frighteningly rapid succession, with little time to fulfill each task with thoroughness and satisfaction. The shocked directors of the LPGA spent much of the first three days trying vociferously to discourage Charlie from fulfilling her plan, and she alternated between feeling guilty and being unreasonably upset that they couldn't accept her wishes.

"The organization doesn't own me, Dad," she complained bitterly, after another lengthy telephone session. "They're actually insisting my fans will think I've *betrayed* them! Why would they? I didn't say I was quitting for *good* !" Throwing a book across the room, she paced the floor, allowing her anger to take over her ability to think rationally.

"Don't let their rhetoric get to you, honey," Jim

cautioned her. "They're only doing their job. You have to live your own life. Everyone will understand in time. Keep your chin up. It's almost over."

But it wasn't. Not by a long shot. The press corps was equally stunned, and its questions incessant and tough. Sportwriters from several national papers and magazines accused her of being spoiled and of using star tactics to hold out for bigger and better stakes. Dozens of phone calls kept her explaining to friends on the tour that she had no ulterior motives other than a year off to rest and to rethink her priorities.

The day before Jim Summers was due to fly to Manzanillo, Charlie was tired of the whole ordeal. Pale and drawn from lack of sleep, even she could tell that she had lost several pounds with the loss of appetite and constantly interrupted meals. However bravely she insisted she could handle the situation, however, the telltale shadows under her red-rimmed eyes at breakfast said otherwise.

"Charlie, we're closing up this house, and you're coming with me tomorrow. I'll call Cortez and explain. You can stay in Mexico long enough for this nonsense to blow over. We'll compose a nice, rational letter of explanation to send to anyone interested in your decision, and ask for understanding, respect, and patience. We'll leave copies with the LPGA and your agent. Later, you can have your writer friend at *Golf Digest* do an interview. That should satisfy the curiosity of all those vultures at our door."

Charlie drew circles on the tablecloth. She hated herself for vacillating so often. Was this the way a newly emancipated golf pro began taking charge of her life? "I don't know, Dad. I hate to run away with my tail between my legs."

"You won't be running *from* anything! You'll be walking *toward* that new future you want, with the freedom to make decisions that affect you and your relationship with God. You know, honey, few of us can travel through life alone. We need God's guidance and direction, and if it takes an abrupt stop for spiritual refueling, then we should take it. Be glad that you heard His voice calling to you, and take the necessary time to listen.''

"Oh, Dad." Charlie stopped to clear the waver in her voice with a quick sip of orange juice. "What would I do without you?"

"That question doesn't need an answer," Jim returned gruffly, patting her shoulder. "But I do want to hear your permission to call Cort Ruillon now. Will you come with me tomorrow, and give yourself a break from this barrage of press nitpicking?"

Charlie fidgeted with her napkin, again hesitating and hoping she had the strength to say no. When the persistent ringing of the telephone broke the silence, she raised violet eyes dull with defeat. "Okay, I'll go. But I'll stay for only one week, two at the most."

"You won't regret it, honey girl, and Cort will be delighted." Jim picked up the receiver and placed a finger on the button to disconnect the call.

Charlie watched him place the receiver on the table next to the telephone base, and felt relief wash over her. Although she was trained not to reveal her emotions while battling with competitors, the elements, and even herself, on the golf course . . . she knew if she had to hear the ringing of one more telephone, the request of one more reporter for an interview, the expression of sorrow over her decision from one more friend, she would go stark, raving mad.

Later, in her room, she leaned her head against her windowpane and thought about her faults—her inability to make decisions, her quick temper—and decided they were directly related to her lack of spiritual discipline. At twenty-six, she was a seasoned traveler in her capacity as the darling of women's professional golf, but had evidently seen it—and herself—through

rose-colored glasses. Her interests had been unbelievably narrow, and her viewpoint of herself shamefully
myopic. She had never minded the ringing telephones
nor the pursuit of fans and press before—not when
their messages sang her praises—but look at her now!
After a scant two weeks of written and verbalized
criticism from those same fans and writers, she was
on the verge of a nervous breakdown!

*My intentions are admirable, Lord. I just want to
take full charge of my life for the first time, and stop
being "managed" by Dad, and my agent and the
LPGA officials. I need to make changes that will
enrich my life and bring it into proper balance . . .
and learning to control my temper is high on the list. I
want to release Dad from feeling even partially
responsible for my happiness, too. I thought I could
do that with one swift chop, but now I've bungled the
effort, and he's more concerned than ever.*

*If I stay here, I'll give in to my vanity and return to
golf for all the wrong reasons. Temptation comes in
many disguises, doesn't it? I'm not very good at
resisting temptation, and I still make a lot of unnecessary mistakes before remembering to turn to You for
guidance. While I'm at it, Lord, I might as well ask
You to bless my future host. I have no reason to doubt
Dad's belief that I'm welcome to accompany him to
Mexico, but in my present mental condition, I can't
help imagining his friend Cort's reticence.*

While packing her suitcases, Charlie felt her heart
lighten considerably. Traveling with her father had
always been a pleasant experience. Like it or not,
Cortez Ruillon would have another house guest.

CHAPTER 2

CHARLIE MADE A MEAGER BREAKFAST for Jim and herself—toast, jam, and instant coffee. It was too early for anything else, and the airline would serve something more substantial. She finished packing immediately after clearing up the kitchen. With nothing more to do until the cab arrived to take them to the airport, she wandered aimlessly through the house.

One or two weeks more in the company of her father wouldn't hurt. She was still determined to give him his complete freedom, but all things considered, it would be easier to initiate a clean break from a neutral place where neither of them would be surrounded by memories of the past.

Walking to the window of the study, Charlie peered out over the small backyard bordered by a weathered cedar fence. It was almost covered with the growth of climbing roses, and offered a steady and faithful supply of cheerful color to the otherwise drab terrain in the desert community. The scene evoked pictures of happier days when she and her father had shared

28

suppers after hard practice sessions. She sighed dejectedly.

"Charlie?" Her father entered the study, and she turned guiltily from her reminiscing. "Are you ready to go?"

She caught the look of concern on his face, and smiled brightly. "All set. Looks like it's going to be a beautiful day."

"Do you wish you were spending it on the golf course? Is that what that wistful sigh was all about?"

"Heavens, no! I'm not even going to *think* about golf for the next two weeks. I was inspecting the yard. Did Mr. Devlin agree to keep it in good condition while we're away? I'd hate to see all that beauty die from lack of attention."

"Yes. I spoke with Devlin last evening. His wife will continue to clean the house as often as necessary, and he'll tend the yard, even if you return later on. I don't want you to be concerned with housekeeping on your . . . *vacation*." Jim smiled at her with familiar indulgence.

"You continue to spoil me, Dad. I've never been much help to you. Come to think of it, I've lived out of a suitcase or on the fairways so long, I know very little about running a home. I remember Nancy Lopez saying her mother never allowed her to wash the dishes for fear the water would soften her hands and ruin her grip. You've been that protective of me, too."

"Don't fret about it, honey. When the time comes, you'll learn housekeeping skills quickly."

The sound of the doorbell stifled Charlie's reply, and she cast an impatient glance at her watch. "That can't be the cab, Dad. It's not due for another thirty minutes. You don't think it's one more reporter, do you? Why can't the pests take a simple no for an answer!"

"Don't worry yourself into another headache,

Charlie. I'll get rid of whoever it is. Sit down and relax." Jim patted her arm and strode from the room.

In a couple minutes, he returned, a flicker of guilt crossing his face when he presented their visitor. "Look who's here, Charlie. I told Dean our cab is due any minute, but he insisted on seeing you first. I'll carry our bags out to the front steps while you talk."

Dean Connally watched her father leave the room before turning to face her. It was their first confrontation since the ill-fated night of their broken engagement, and Charlie, still smarting from Dean's accusation, struggled to maintain a degree of aloofness.

"Hello, Charlie." A warm pink flush spread over Dean's face when he met her steady gaze. "I wanted to see you before you left."

"What about?" She knew she was being petulant, but she simply couldn't make it easy for him. Merely looking at him put her on the defensive.

"I hated to see you leave town without apologizing to you, Charlie." His clear blue eyes searched her face. "I haven't had a minute's peace of mind since . . . that night. My behavior was out of line. I'm sorry. I know I hurt you."

"Please, Dean, there's nothing to be gained by dwelling on the past."

He frowned. "I guess it's asking too much of you. If only I hadn't made such a mess of things . . . if I had been more patient." Charlie knew it was costing him a great deal to seek her forgiveness, and felt herself responding to the husky emotion in his voice.

"We were both at fault, Dean. Please don't take all the blame. It was for the best, anyway."

Dean looked puzzled. "For the best? I don't understand."

Charlie sighed. "Our engagement should never have taken place, Dean. The love I had for you was really that of a sister for a brother. That's the reason I found it so difficult to return the passion you wanted from me. I enjoyed being with you, sharing experiences and aspirations, but I never really felt . . . romantic.''

Dean closed the space between them in a rush, and clasped her hands tightly in his. "How can you say that? What we had was wonderful. It can be again. We'll start over, Charlie. I've never stopped loving you. I even have the ring. . . .'' He reached into his shirt pocket and pulled out the diamond solitare, pushing it into her hand. "I never meant to give it to anyone else. It's yours to keep.''

Summoning all her strength, Charlie pushed it away and moved toward the door. "I don't want the ring back. It's over, Dean. At least that part of our relationship is. I hope we can remain good friends, though. We've shared too many important events in our lives.'' She made a pointed effort to check her watch, hoping he would take the hint and leave. "It was good of you to come. We needed to have this meeting behind us.''

Dean hesitated only a few seconds before continuing. "I know you feel you need to punish me a while longer, Charlie. I deserve to be, so I'll be patient this time. You have resigned from the pro tour as I always wanted you to do, and I don't have the right to ask for anything more right now. Take your vacation in Mexico, and I'll wait until you return to give back your ring. It belongs on your finger, darling.''

"Please, Dean, I don't *want* you to wait for me. I might not return for a long time.'' Charlie became increasingly frustrated. Didn't he understand?

"Charlie, the cab is here.'' The interruption from her father was so welcome she almost flung her arms around his neck. Only his look of concern kept her from doing so.

"I'll get my purse, Dad. Goodbye, Dean. Thanks again for coming over.'' She flashed him a fleeting smile and dashed from the room.

"Goodbye, darling. Write if you find the time." His cheerful reply followed her into the hall. It was hopeless. He simply hadn't heard a single word she'd said. Before she left Mexico, she would write him a letter. Perhaps he would finally accept the fact that there was no future for them as a married couple when he saw it in black and white. If she had sought God's purpose in her life from the very beginning, she would have understood the importance of finding a mate who could walk beside her, and move in the same direction toward their respective goals.

From this moment on, she intended to return God to His proper place in her life. She had put too many other things first, and it had cost her the peace of mind she had once experienced when first surrendering to Him. Her husband, whoever he might be, would have to be someone who shared that commitment.

Charlie dallied in her room longer than necessary, and was relieved to find Dean gone when she reached the front door. "Sorry, Dad," she apologized.

Jim locked the door behind them and pocketed the key. "It seems strange to see you going somewhere without a golf bag slung over your shoulder, Charlie. You're sure you don't want your clubs? Two weeks is a long time."

"I'm positive. I intend to read, swim, and sleep . . . period."

Jim laughed. "If you can do that for even two days, I'll eat my favorite fishing hat."

"With or without onions?" Charlie countered, before climbing into the cab. As it pulled away from the curb, she saw a television press van from a local station approaching from the opposite direction. She smiled with smug satisfaction and relaxed against the stiff vinyl seat. She had made a wise decision.

Cortez Ruillon had arranged for a resort van to meet them at the airport. Charlie quietly observed the loading of their luggage, and then piled onto a middle seat next to her father. As they drove carefully over a narrow serpentine road past acres of coconut palms, climbing steadily until glimpses of Manzanillo Bay overwhelmed her with its beauty, she became fully conscious of where she was, and why. Suddenly, the idea of barging in on an unknown host brought an attack of the jitters.

"Dad, exactly what did you tell Mr. Ruillon, and exactly what was his response?" she questioned aloud.

Jim glanced at her briefly before peering out the window again. "Relax, Charlie. Isn't this place gorgeous? A person could get spoiled waking up to such lush green . . ."

"Dad, please! I want to know," she insisted, with an unnecessarily sharp edge in her voice.

"Take it easy, honey," Jim soothed. "I merely said your plans had changed and asked if you could come along. He said that was fine."

"That's it? He didn't want to know why I was coming He didn't ask any questions about me at all?"

"Charlie, really, you worry too much about details. Cort is my friend, remember? If I ask a small favor of him, he isn't going to refuse me."

"That's the problem. You put him on the spot and he had no choice!" She shot him a troubled glance.

"You'll be as welcome as rain in a drought, Charlie. You'll see."

Charlie sighed. Apparently she wouldn't get any more information or the least bit of sympathy from her father. Fidgeting nervously with her sunglasses, and needing the calming effects of conversation to quiet her restlessness, she turned to Jim again.

"Tell me about this place of Cort's, Dad."

"To tell you the truth, honey, I don't have the vocabulary to describe it. It's called *Las Hadas*, and as the name translates, it is indeed a fairyland. You'll

33

swear you're seeing a page torn from *The Arabian Nights*. The resort was built by a Bolivian tin baron as the ultimate hideaway for his jet-set friends, but they weren't faithful about returning in the years after its sensational opening gala, and he had to give up his playland. He sold it to Cort's conglomerate, and with his marketing know-how, he's made it into a popular facility for the affluent. He has ambitious plans to develop the thousand-plus acres surrounding it on Santiago Peninsula. I'm sure he'll tell us all about it."

Quite abruptly the driver swung around a hair-raising curve and Las Hadas lay before them, sprawling over the cliffs above the Bay—a dazzling concoction of domes and towers, shining under the hot Mexican sun. The Moorish-Mediterranean architecture was extravagant in its use of cupolas and turrets, with breathtaking results. The deliberate and fanciful use of stark white exteriors made the lavish landscaping all the more effective in its contrast, and everywhere, startling masses of bougainvilleas burst with scarlet blooms, tumbling from the hillside and room balconies.

"It's incredible!" gasped Charlie. "You're sure this isn't a dream? It's an absolute . . . paradise."

Jim smiled at her rapture. "I'm glad you're here to see it. Most of us live with the idea that perfection can only be achieved in our dreams, or by one of God's miracles, and then we see something like this. It's nice to know a mere man can build something so nearly perfect, isn't it?"

The driver took them past the entrance to the mystical resort, though, and continued along a narrow road hugging the steep hills. He made a sharp turn and headed toward an equally awesome white villa, perched at the very edge of a cliff, resplendent with its own share of elaborate peaks and whorls. From its vantage point, the villa had an exalted panorama of the sea, the sand, and the sun-kissed fairyland called Las Hadas.

There wasn't time for Charlie to speculate about the owner of all this luxury. Before the van came to a complete stop, two *djellaba*-clad servants ran down the white marble steps from the entrance to greet them and take charge of their luggage. Instantly Jim was assisting her out of the vehicle, an astonishingly visible eagerness in his movements. He was more excited about beginning his new career than she had fully realized.

Halfway up the wide crystalline stairs, Charlie saw her host emerge from the doorway. Unconsciously, she pulled back to walk a step or two behind her father.

Over six feet tall, with broad muscular shoulders and narrow hips, Cortez Ruillon had the unmistakable look of an aristocrat, lord of all he surveyed. Thick, crisp black hair glistened under the sun's harsh brilliance, and set off his equally dark, deep-set eyes. High cheekbones and a square jaw were chiseled into devastating angles under his taut mahogany skin. When he moved toward Jim with long, loose-limbed strides and flashed a rakish white smile of welcome, Charlie stopped breathing entirely, and felt her heart thump wildly somewhere in her throat. He was the most devilishly handsome man she had ever seen.

"Jim! It's good to have you here at last, my friend." Fascinated, Charlie watched bulging muscles ripple under his white silk shirt when he gripped her father's hand. She felt herself straining for the sound of his distinctive baritone voice with its slight accent.

"I told you when the time was right, I'd come, Cort." Jim grinned and slapped his new mentor affectionately on the back. "I'm glad you still wanted me. Hope I can live up to your expectations."

"I deal with only the best, Jim. Not for one minute do I expect you to disappoint me."

"It was nice of you to let Charlie come along. You remember her, don't you?" Her father had turned only halfway in her direction to make the introduction, when Charlie saw that his attention had been diverted. She followed his gaze to the open doorway where a beautiful dark-haired woman and a young boy stood waiting. The woman smiled and held out both her hands in welcome.

"Hello, Jim. How are you?" The richly modulated contralto voice reached out beyond Jim to encompass Charlie. She continued to watch the woman, completely mesmerized.

Jim walked over to her at once, took both her proffered hands in his, and held them while they talked, though Charlie couldn't hear what they were saying. The young boy spoke then, and her father bent to extend a formal handshake, before ruffling his hair affectionately. Charlie swallowed convulsively. That one heartrending, tender gesture spoke volumes.

"Do you feel left out?"

At the sound of the low, deep voice, Charlie turned abruptly and raised startled eyes to meet the darkly probing ones of Cortez Ruillon. In the sunlight, the severely contracted black pupils of his eyes were piercing and omniscient. Even the liquid sheen of deep coffee-brown irises surrounding them failed to dispel the sensation of undefined dangers lurking beneath their surface.

"L-left out?" she stuttered, struggling to regain her poise. Not for anything would she let this arrogantly cool man know she had felt like an intruder on her father's privacy, and not left out of his touching reunion with friends. "I don't understand," she continued, forcing a slightly husky laugh from her throat. Was he insinuating there was some relationship between her father and his sister that she didn't know about?

"Oh, I think you know what I meant . . . Charlie." The intimacy in Ruillon's low-pitched voice created havoc with her nerves. "My sister is lovely, isn't she?"

His dark gaze left her face and took its time inspecting her from head to toe as she stood with her hands in the pockets of her man-tailored slacks. Charlie lifted her chin a little higher, and balled her hands into fists inside the pockets. When Ruillon's gaze returned to lock with hers, his eyes glittered with undisguised interest.

"For some reason, I expected you to have married and left the nest by now, Miss Summers. Quitting the tour because Jim finally consented to design a course for me and then following him down here wasn't the wisest decision you could have made. He's going to be a busy man and won't have much time to entertain you. Furthermore, you should know that I won't brook any interference while he's working for me."

Charlie bristled at the total inaccuracy of Ruillon's words. She had an almost uncontrollable urge to wipe the mocking look from his face with the full force of her putting iron, and that surprised her. While she was temperamental at times, she had never considered herself a violent person. She struggled for a measure of self-composure.

"My goodness, Señor Ruillon!" she exclaimed, attempting to be charming but inwardly seething. "Whatever are you talking about? I wouldn't think of disrupting my father's work, and he wouldn't let me, I assure you. If you check again, you'll learn that I resigned from the tour *before* I knew Dad's plans, and *he* was the one who insisted I accompany him here for a couple weeks. I didn't want to come, and I have no intention of getting in his way. He'll feel dreadful when I tell him he was mistaken in believing I would be welcome here." Charlie met Cort's gaze head on before turning with the quick, athletic grace so highly touted by the press.

A firm grasp of her elbow brought her up close to Cortez Ruillon's boldly masculine body, and the contact sent electrifying shocks throughout her network of nerves. Again, his low taunting voice reached only her ears. He was taking care that no one hear their strange verbal encounter. "That was a clever bluff, but then you've had a few more years than most daughters to practice your technique of manipulating Daddy, haven't you? At least twenty-five, I'd say. We'll leave things as they are. You and I can settle this on our own."

Charlie had difficulty with her breathing once more. She didn't really like this egocentric friend of her father, yet she seemed to be responding to his nearness as she never had with Dean Connally.

"Are we in agreement, Charlie?" The velvety deep tones of his voice weakened her resistance, and her thick naturally dark lashes fluttered upward, allowing their eyes to lock briefly before he gently released his grip on her tingling arm. "Charlie . . ." he frowned, repeating her name. "Why do you have a man's name?"

"It's a nickname. . . . Dad gave it to me," she defended stiffly, daring him to find fault with it. "My full name is Charline."

Cortez arched one eyebrow, his eyes continuing to hold her captive. "I like Charlie better. It's so deliciously incongruous." His eyes raked her figure again, and the mocking smile returned to his full lips. "You don't look anything like a man."

At a loss for words, Charlie abruptly mounted the steps. *Dear Lord, don't let me fall for him*, she prayed fervently; but even as she finished the earnest plea, she turned for one more quick glance at the man whose voice and eyes left her dizzy.

CHAPTER 3

CHARLIE TAPPED HER FATHER'S SHOULDER and peeked around at him with twinkling eyes. "Hi, Dad. Remember me?"

Jim chuckled and drew her into the circle of his arm. "Forgive me, honey. I'd like you to meet Cort's sister, Marita Ruillon de Granado, and her son, Alejandro. Marita and I have known each other for several years, but it has been a good two and a half since our last meeting."

The brief and understated introduction revealed nothing about the reason for the conspicuous warmth in Jim's voice, but eager to convey her approval of any interest he might have in Marita, Charlie greeted her with enthusiasm. "Hello, Señora Granado, I'm happy to meet you. If you're a friend of my father, than you must be a very special person. I hope we can be friends, too." She extended her hand, knowing that as soon as the words passed her lips, she meant them.

"Thank you. I'd like that." Marita smiled the words, and at once Charlie was conscious of another

39

beauty the woman possessed—the beauty of naturalness; a radiant inner beauty of contentment that exuded without conscious effort from her face, her voice, her inherent refinement.

"You must call me Marita, and . . . may I call you Charlie? That is how I've known you from your father."

"I'll insist on it, Marita. And how about you, Alejandro? Have you a special nickname?" Charlie smiled engagingly at the boy, liking the alert flash of interest in his dark luminous eyes, and admiring his uncommon patience in waiting out the introductions without a fuss. She mentally calculated his age at nine or ten.

"No, *señorita*, I am only Alejandro, after my father." There was intense pride in his young voice, and a determination to give the revered name its deserved honor. He took her fingers to his lips, bowing in perfect mimicry of an older Spanish gentleman.

For an instant, Charlie imagined his uncle teaching him this formal method of greeting, and wondered if she would have trembled as much as she had before if *he* had chosen to greet her in the same way. She'd never have the opportunity to find out, however. She couldn't imagine the pompous Cortez Ruillon bowing to her for even the sake of customary politeness. He had made her an enemy already, from preconceived ideas based solely on suppositions, and he hadn't wasted a single second in letting her know.

Pushing the unwelcome interest in the uncle to the back of her mind, Charlie's smile returned, and expanded. "If I had a beautiful name like Alejandro, I wouldn't want it shortened, either." She cocked her head and pretended to look him over critically. "Besides, you look exactly like an Alejandro, and not anything like an Ali!"

"Thank you, *señorita*." He rewarded her with a wide, white grin.

"Do you suppose," Charlie continued in a chatty, conspiratorial tone, "that if we get permission from your mother, you might call me Charlie, rather than *señorita*? If we're going to be pals, it has to be on a first-name basis for both of us, don't you agree?"

Alejandro nodded eagerly, but looked to his mother for the needed approval. "Mama?"

"All right, dear, but don't abuse the privilege."

Charlie winked with a conspicuously broad facial grimace, rubbed her hands together dramatically, slapped the right palm against her hard, lean thigh, and thrust it forward, saying, "Put 'er there, pal!"

Alejandro watched in fascination, hesitated only a few seconds, and then copied her actions with youthful verve. "Put 'er there, pal!"

Everyone laughed, enjoying the game Charlie had employed to win the boy's confidence, but Charlie's pleasure came to an abrupt halt when a familiar deep voice ordered, "Go show your new pal her room, Alejandro. I'm sure she wants to get out of this hot sun and wash up. We'll be in the garden room having refreshments."

Charlie felt her cheeks burning. She was being dismissed from Ruillon's presence—from the company of other adults—like some naughty child being sent to her room for punishment. Was he daring her to make a scene and thereby prove his theory . . . that she was spoiled and immature?

"Please, Marita, I'd enjoy having Alejandro for a guide. He can give me a mini-tour of this fascinating villa on the way. The three of you undoubtedly have memories to talk about, and probably some blank spaces to fill in, as well. We'll join you later." Pulling out all the stops for charm, Charlie slanted an ingenuous glance at her host. "There *will* be juice and cookies for us when we get back, won't there, *señor?*"

Ruillon's eyes glittered threateningly for a brief

second before he also shrugged nonchalantly. "Certainly, *señorita* , and milk, also."

"Oh, good!" she retorted gleefully through clenched teeth. "Athletes and children need several glasses of milk a day. It's very beneficial." She turned from his glowering look to hook her hand through Alejandro's arm, but immensely pleased with her ability to match Ruillon's verbal thrusts, couldn't resist a whispered gibe in passing. "I believe that makes 'par.' "

Why was Cortez Ruillon so determined to upset her? Well, she might be younger than her host, and most certainly less experienced, but with her status as a professional athlete in the world of women's sports came a wealth of poise under pressure. Women who couldn't take the rigorous strain were weeded out rather quickly. *She* had made it to the top. *She* was a winner, a *consistent* winner. That was the goal of any professional—to be first among equals. She'd show Ruillon gamesmanship!

They had climbed to the top of a sweeping, white marble stairway, and Alejandro led her to a door halfway down a wide hall of whitewashed rough plaster, hung with oversized paintings splashed with brilliant rainbow colors. Charlie would have continued further, except for the impatient tug on her hand.

"No, Charlie, this is your room." Alejandro pushed open an intricately carved door and gestured. "See?"

"You're absolutely right, Alejandro. Those are my suitcases. I knew I couldn't go wrong, if you were my guide." Grateful for the distraction he was providing from her incomprehensible confusion about Ruillon, she continued her banter.

"Let's see now . . ." She was startled by the beauty of the understated and luxurious guest room. Everything—walls, ceiling, marble floor, area carpet, furniture, drapes, and spread—was stark white. The only color came from three large paintings, a giant bouquet of fresh flowers on a long dresser, and the glorious view of the bay and Las Hadas tucked away on the cliffs above it. Charlie gasped her pleasure.

"Do you like it, Charlie?" Alejandro hadn't stopped grinning.

"It's perfect . . . and when a guide gives such wonderful service, he should be properly rewarded. If you are patient while I open this suitcase . . ." She lifted the largest of them to the bench at the foot of the king-size bed, and unzipped the lid.

Alejandro's eyes grew larger in anticipation, and he moved close beside her to peer inside while she dug beneath neatly folded slacks and blouses.

"Uh-huh, I thought so. I've got two. One for you and one for me. Now everyone will know we're pals for sure." She pulled out two bright red baseball caps, and handed one to him.

"Gosh! Thanks a lot, Charlie!" Alejandro beamed his gratitude, pulling on the cap and fitting it far forward over his eyes. He tilted his head straight backward in order to see her face. "I always wanted one of these. I like baseball very much. Mama lets me see it on television sometimes, and I've tried it in school."

"I wear my hat when I'm golfing. It shields my eyes from the sun. But, you should wear it a little farther back on your head. See. Like this." She adjusted her own, and then took a swing with an imaginary golf club. "Do you know how to play golf, pal?"

"No, but I would like to learn."

"I'll . . . *my father* will be glad to teach you while he's here." She had almost volunteered to do it herself, but remembered in time that she had no intention of staying long enough to give any golf lessons.

Suddenly she felt tired. There was no sense in psyching herself up to do further battle with Cortez Ruillon. With only a day—she knew she must leave tomorrow—in which to enjoy this enchanting white fairyland, she should avoid conflict at all costs. Looking for faults in others and bearing grudges because of them defeated the purpose of her professional hiatus. Only yesterday she had reread the verse in Proverbs which reminded her that, "Pride goeth before destruction, and an haughty spirit before a fall." It would take all the divine grace she could appropriate to control her tongue . . . especially where her temporary host was concerned. For some reason, she felt out of control in his presence, but she knew that the anger and sarcasm that seemed to pour from her lips were inexcusable ways of dealing with her shortcomings.

Once again, a verse from Proverbs came unbidden, and she smiled to herself. "He that is slow to anger is better than the mighty." If she were honest with herself, she would admit that she was not Cortez Ruillon's equal. She was entirely out of her element with him. He was not only older, but more experienced in every way. He had once been married. He looked for mature qualities in women, and he had been able to sense her naïveté at a glance, and probably the same flawed qualities Dean had accused her of possessing.

Sighing deeply, Charlie pulled a fresh blouse from the suitcase. If only Cort had greeted her with the same warmth shown to her father, flashed her a rakish smile and bent his dark head over her hand . . . he was undoubtedly a polished gentleman in his dealings with women. No, she was no match at all for someone like him. Still, there was no harm in daydreaming.

"What are you doing, Charlie?"

Startled by Alejandro's question, she flushed as red as his hat, and yanked the visor down over his eyes to prevent him from seeing her embarrassment. Thank goodness, he was still too young to understand the ways of a fanciful young woman.

"Excuse me a second, pal. I'm going to change my blouse and wash up a bit. Then we'll go down for those promised cookies. Okay?"

"*Si, señorita* . . . I mean Charlie." Alejandro grinned shyly. Sitting on the edge of the bed, he removed his hat to examine the emblem above its visor.

In the equally splendid bathroom, Charlie splashed her face with cold water, and chuckled over her incredible display of fantasy. Fortunately the boy's uncle hadn't witnessed such nonsense. How he would have laughed.

Why did her thoughts keep returning to him? She disliked him without knowing why; yet she was eager to get back downstairs. Would he continue to tease her about her name? Would he make her feel welcome this time?

A strange stirring of her senses made her breathless in anticipation. It was not an unpleasant feeling.

Even before she and Alejandro neared the garden room, the sound of shared laughter echoed throughout the spacious house. Unconsciously Charlie quickened her steps, both in curiosity over what had triggered the infectious mirth, and in hopes of catching a glimpse of Cortez Ruillon at total ease, his heart-stopping smile flashing, and his dark, smoldering eyes brilliant with merriment.

So eager were her expectations, her violet eyes bypassed the closeness of her father to Marita Granado, the casual presence of her hand on his forearm, and zoomed with pinpoint precision to feast on the swarthy features of Cortez.

It was a breath-snatching experience . . . but the sensation was short-lived. As though a silent alarm had warned him of her presence the second she crossed the threshold, he instantaneously sobered, a deep scowl dousing any residual flash of merriment from his eyes. His disapproval was obvious, a cold

45

and deliberate reinforcement of his previous message—she was an outsider here, unwelcome.

She straightened her backbone, and spoke with almost shrill gaiety. "We're back, everybody, dying of thirst and ready for those promised treats!" She placed one arm loosely around Alejandro's shoulders, both for moral support, and to steady herself. Her legs were stricken with a sudden case of the wobbles.

Ignoring Ruillon's dark gaze, she smiled at his sister. "Your son makes a wonderful guide, Marita. You can be proud of him."

"I am. I thank God daily for loaning him to me." Marita responded with an answering smile encompassing them both. "Are you pleased with your room, Charlie?"

"I would have to be blind not to enjoy such extravagant beauty. Do you ever tire of the view?" Charlie caught the gesture from her father to join him on the couch, and slid onto the seat beside him, grateful for the opportunity to sit. Her legs were still trembling.

"I'm embarrassed to admit that every so often I crave the harsh and haunting beauty of ice and snow. When the desire is strong enough, I fly to the nearest mountain snowfall. Why, Alejandro, dear, where did you get that fine new hat?" Marita held out her arms for her young son, and he went into them hesitantly, explaining all the way.

"From Charlie, Mama. She's got one, too, because we're pals. I didn't ask for it, honest. She gave it to me."

"I hope you remembered to say thank you."

"I did, Mama. I wouldn't forget." He threw Charlie an apprehensive glance.

"Your thank-you was the nicest one I've ever received, Alejandro." She was given an exaggerated sigh of relief, and laughed huskily.

Charlie knew her host was standing beside the

portable refreshment cart waiting for her drink preference, but since she was still undecided about how to handle his taunting, she stalled for time by continuing her conversation with Marita. "Are you responsible for the lovely interior decoration in the villa? It has such perfect rapport with the total environment. I love it!"

"I wish I could take the credit, Charlie, but it must all go to Cort. It has been his pet project over the past few years."

Charlie realized she had just propelled herself into a situation as tricky and maddening as stroking her golf ball into a sand bunker on the eighteenth hole in a tie game. It was unnerving, to say the least, but it was her move. The gallery was waiting.

Squashing the nervous convulsion in her stomach, she pushed up the corners of her mouth into a bright smile and met the amused gaze of her host. Quickly she breathed a short prayer for help. "Congratulations, Señor Ruillon," she crooned, "you have created an artistic masterpiece." She attempted to keep her voice deliberately casual, but the man's mere presence caused her heart to pound. His smile was devastating.

"Thank you. You're very kind." Ruillon's air of total indifference was maddening. Was he mocking her again? "If we're to live as one family at Las Hadas, Charlie, isn't it about time you called me Cort?" He raised one heavy eyebrow in challenge before handing Alejandro a glass of fruit juice.

"It's your castle, *señor*, and your wish is my command. Cort it shall be." Charlie felt her father's look of surprise, and wished she had bitten her tongue before emitting the flippant reply. If she weren't careful, he would demand an explanation, and she didn't have one.

"Good. Now if you'll give me your drink preference, Charlie, we can toast Jim's arrival and success

47

here at Las Hadas. We're drinking mango juice, and you can have that or . . ." Cort grinned as he held up a small pitcher of milk.

"Cort, dear, stop your teasing," Marita chided her brother. "In case you haven't noticed, Charlie is a mature young woman."

"I've noticed several things about Charlie, Marita." His reply was bland enough, but Charlie grew increasingly flustered.

"I'll have mango juice, please. I need something tall and cool after that long trip from the airport." She ignored his attempt at humor, but not the brief contact between his long, lean fingers and her clammy ones in the passing of the glass. Was she *that* disturbed by him? It didn't make sense. She had grown up in an adult world, educated to meet new challenges head-on . . and her life had always involved working with men of all ages . . . but, for some inexplicable reason, in Cort's presence, she felt like Alejandro's contemporary.

Charlie's thoughts came to a crashing close with a not-too-gentle nudge from her father's knee. Her eyes flashed from face to face. What were they waiting for?

"Evidently your daughter doesn't share our sentiments, Jim. Perhaps she thinks your success here will keep you from returning to Palm Springs." Cort's voice was as cold as his carved-in-bronze features when he raised his glass in a silent salute to Jim Summers.

Charlie's heart gave a sickening lurch. She had missed the toast! Better not admit she had been daydreaming. "You're too quick with your judgments, Cort. I wanted to add something of my own before I joined you in yours." As soon as the words left her mouth, a stab of guilt compounded her misery. There was no reason for her to indulge in deceit.

She turned to her father and raised her glass. "It's time for you to test your advice to me these past several years, Dad. *Singlemindedness* is the key word. Remember? Concentrate on building your golf course. Nothing else—no one else—is important right now. I believe in you. I'm proud of you. I love you. Don't ever forget it."

Her last words were only a whisper, the lump in her throat making any further sounds impossible. Later, her father would understand she had been saying goodbye to him. He would know—and Cort would know—she wanted him to begin a new life without her at the core.

"Thank you, honey. I knew I could count on you." Jim clicked her glass and then raised his to the others in the room. "I'll give it my best shot. Thanks for your confidence in me. It means a great deal." He sipped from the rim of his glass and threw a quick assessing glance at Charlie.

"Finish your refreshments, Jim, and I'll take you up to your room." Cort's voice was amiable. "You might want to change into something more comfortable. There're still a couple of hours of good daylight, and I thought you'd enjoy a tour around the area we've reserved for the course. I've got a Land Rover outside."

"Now you're talking, boss. That's why I'm here. The sooner we get started, the better." Jim rose from the couch and moved spryly to place his empty glass on the beverage cart.

"You don't have to sound quite so happy, Jim. You've been less than an hour in my presence, and already you're eager to get away. I can see I'll need to take extra care dressing for dinner tonight, or I'll spend it listening to a dreary recital of your tour." Marita pouted at the two men, but her soft contralto voice was rich with teasing inflections. A halo of black curls framed her oval face, flawlessly molded with smooth, silky skin. She was youthfully vivacious, and apparently not afraid to go after what she wanted.

Jim self-consciously ran nervous fingers through his thick sandy hair. "It would be impossible to ignore you, Marita."

Marita tucked a hand into the bend of Jim's elbow, and held out the full skirt of her colorfully embroidered dress with the other to drop a curtsy. "Thank you, kind sir. I wasn't asking for that lovely statement, but it was . . . delightful." She pulled him gently across the room, throwing a rebellious look at her brother. "I will take Jim to his room, Cort. I can't have all my duties as your hostess usurped."

"Can I go show Julio and Sarita my new hat, Mama?" Alejandro was quick to recognize an opportunity to leave.

"Yes, but watch the time carefully, son. You are to eat supper in the kitchen with Delfina tonight."

"*Si*, I won't forget. See you later, Charlie." He was already running from the room.

"If you wait an extra second, I'll come up with you, too, Dad. I need to check on a couple things before you go off on your tour." Charlie spoke calmly enough, but her heart tripped nearer the edge of panic. Not for a fortune in tacos would she remain alone with Cortez Ruillon! Without as much as a glance in his direction, she pushed her empty juice glass onto the drink cart, and started after the couple lingering by the door.

A steel vise closed over her wrist. "Wait, Charlie. Go ahead, you two. She'll be along in a minute."

"Go ahead, Dad. The master of Las Hadas has spoken. If I don't obey, he might throw me to the sharks out in the bay, and I have my heart set on sleeping in that heavenly king-size bed upstairs!"

Marita's soft laughter rolled from her throat. "I adore your sense of humor, Charlie. You have a unique flair for the dramatic. When these two men of ours have escaped to the hills, we will get together for some girl talk."

50

"I'd like that, Marita. Come to my room when you're ready."

Until the sounds of footsteps and laughter reached mid-stairs, Charlie made no attempt to free herself from Cort's hold on her wrist.

"What are you trying to pull, Charlie? Aren't you a little old to interfere in your father's private life?" Cort's low-pitched voice was dangerously soft, and the breath from each word he spoke parted the golden strands of her hair. Obviously he believed her toast to Jim had been a warning to stick to his job and leave Marita alone.

Charlie stiffened at his implication, repeated now for the second time since her arrival. Evidently she had two strikes against her. Cort thought she had purposely resigned from the LPGA to follow her father to Mexico and discourage his interest in beginning a new, independent career; and now, sensing her father's possible interest in Marita, was attempting to warn him against such an alliance before it was even launched. She was innocent of both charges! The urge to fight back ballooned but since she owed Cort no explanations, she refused to turn around to face him. She couldn't anyway. She'd crumble under his stony gaze.

She could hear the harsh rhythm of his breathing mere inches above her ear. "I'm waiting."

"You'll have to wait a long time, Cort," she mumbled mutinously. "Golf is the only game I play." Her pulse fluttered alarmingly in her throat, but she didn't budge.

"Who said we were playing a game?"

Charlie steeled herself against the mellowness of Cort's voice and the continued warmth of his hand on her wrist. More than ever, she needed to get away from his closeness before it was too late, but she had indicated her course of action and she wouldn't back down. "Wh—what would you call it then?"

51

"Turn around, Charlie. I refuse to talk to the back of your head another minute." His free hand settled on the curve of her waist, threatening a further possession of her will. The warmth emanating from its pressure made it easier to imagine herself in his arms, and in in spite of her verbal protests, she knew that's what she wanted more than anything else.

Flirting with further danger, she taunted, "Did you push your wife around, Cort? Since she died, do you have to browbeat defenseless women about imagined problems?"

Instantaneously he released her wrist and stepped in front of her, the anger visible in his face, a living thing, ready to erupt at any moment from its intensity. His nostrils flared above the thin line of his mouth. "That was totally uncalled for!" he rasped, his fury barely contained. "Do you always make such snap judgments?" Cort was in full control again, though his voice was barely more than a whisper.

A succumbing weakness crept along Charlie's limbs, and she slipped her hands inside her pockets. "No more often than you do," she managed to protest. Cort's penetrating gaze held her rigidly in place; she couldn't escape. "May I leave now?"

"No, I'm not through with you yet." His eyes lowered to take in the trembling curves of her full lips, and a new idea seemed to be born. "I haven't had an opportunity to respond to that vile comment of yours."

Cort's intentions frightened Charlie more than his anger. "I was right," she retorted. "You equate your Latin *machismo* with taking what you want when you want it. Well, you've met your match. No one takes anything from *me* without my permission!" She attempted to move around him, but he was quicker than she, and stopped her retreat from the room.

"Maybe it's time someone did, Charlie," he countered, unruffled by her outburst. His hands on her upper arms brought her easily unto his arms. At first Charlie resisted with fierce determination, but her mouth was imprisoned by his. Unleashed, they seemed to consume her, until she was bereft of air and weakened by the intensity of the possession. Yet, it wasn't only Cort's overwhelming dominance that caused her struggles to cease. It was the sudden surrender of her own lips, and the traitorous response ot her entire body to his kiss.

It was crazy and incomprehensible. She disliked Cort and his treatment of her; certainly, he hadn't kept his animosity toward her a secret. Nevertheless, in all her twenty-six years, the kiss or touch of no man had ever made such an assault on her senses. It was a bitter acknowledgment, one she could never voice. She had known instinctively that she wanted Cort's kiss from the moment she first caught sight of him only hours ago, and it had been as thrilling as she had imagined.

Nevertheless, thinking of her vulnerability made her sick inside! To desire a man who had no respect and admiration for her was masochistic, contrary to everything she believed about herself. No woman should allow herself to be unjustly judged. No woman should allow any man to use her for his personal gain or amusement. No woman—especially a Christiam woman—should allow a man to abuse her physically or mentally out of deference to his strength or position. Yet, here she was, seemingly powerless to fight a man intent on forcing her into subordination to his will.

Cort took advantage of Charlie's unintentional submission by adeptly pulling her compliant body closer. Reluctantly, her own hands felt their way across his muscular shoulders, and finally into the crisp black thickness of his hair. Cort responded by wrapping his arms around her in a bone-crushing embrace, making every beat of his heart known to her.

Frightened and shocked by her willful participation, Charlie frantically pushed him away. "*Stop,* Cort!" Her voice was hoarse with panic. She couldn't deal with this wholly new sensation. Somehow it seemed wrong to her. She *knew* it was wrong! This man was her father's friend and she had known him only a few hours!

"What do you think you're doing!" she cried, her eyes wide and full of condemnation.

Cort's eyes narrowed, and a curtain came down so quickly Charlie wondered if she had imagined the tenderness in them only seconds before. She was still in a state of shock, more with her own actions than with the entirely normal kiss.

"You're really something, Charlie," he said in soft amusement. He laughed quietly while drawing her close. "I can't decide if you're seriously overreacting, or merely playing a game of enticement."

Charlie's pulse leaped in response to his nearness. "Please," she whispered on a note of desperation. "Let me go, Cort."

Abruptly Cort stepped aside. "Sorry." He observed her carefully. Suddenly he heaved a lengthy sigh, and his mouth curled in a bitter twist. "If you insist on hanging around Las Hadas to play with your little pal, Alejandro, just plan to stay out of my way, Charlie," he said grimly. "And that goes double for your father. Let him live his own life, in his own way, without interference."

Charlie flinched, and turned to leave. His words stung like a slap in the face. He simply would not believe her. She spoke with icy composure. "Don't worry, Señor Ruillon. I wouldn't stay here if you paid me. I think you're still angry at your wife for dying, and at your brother-in-law for dumping his family on you. Your anger has made you hard . . . and hostile, so you dictate how people around you are to live without ever consulting them about their preferences." Her voice throbbed with deliberate insolence. "Well, no one tells me what to do."

"That's enough, Charlie."

"I'm not through with *you* yet." Stubbornly, she retaliated in equally cold hauteur, echoing his former words. Latin males weren't the only ones with aggressiveness and pride. "Contrary to what you have concluded, my father is as free to make personal decisions as I am to make mine. But, since you don't understand mutual respect between males and females, I'll leave—tomorrow—and make things easier for you."

She took two steps and halted, too wound up to exit the room. "In case you decide to leave this little Shangri-la some day, Cort, you should know there have been some important changes in the real world. *Mature* men have learned to respect women as equals in the United States. Remember? Or have you been away too long? Women there are admired for their intelligence, their talent, and for their ability and willingness to use them in many endeavors . . . even in professional sports. I prefer a world like that. Las Hadas is a beautiful fairyland, but it's being run by an . . . an inhuman despot who has forgotten that people come here to vacation, not to retire permanently from a full life, as *he* apparently has."

"You're talking utter nonsense. I suggest you keep your childish fabrications to yourself."

"Protesteth a man who couldn't recognize the truth if it hit him in the face!" Too late Charlie realized her temper had leaped out of control again, and her accusations were as unfounded and farfetched as his of her.

Charlie wanted to run from the room and seek shelter behind a locked door, but made one last grandstand effort to strengthen her show of independence and personal strength of character. Turning, she threw Cort a look of arrogant disdain. Pride elevated her chin when she saw the compressed line of his jaw and the impatience in his pitch-black eyes. "Thanks for your hospitality, Your Royal Highness!"

She delivered the taunt in a mockingly sweet voice, and dropped a curtsey of equally deriding obeisance, her head bowed to further her act of humility. Then, with her head held high, she marched with deliberate, unhurried strides out the door of the garden room, across the altogether too enormous foyer, and up the wide marble steps.

As she climbed, she heard the unmistakable rumble of deep laughter. It began as a chuckle and built up steadily in volume and endurance until the sound became tumultuous.

Charlie stomped out her frustration and anger on the last remaining steps, and down the corridor to her room. How dare that . . . insolent . . . man laugh at her! If it weren't for her father, she would leave immediately. Why, why, *why* had she ever consented to come to Las Hadas?

Consumed by the fever of her unreasonable rage, Charlie balled her hands into fists and clenched her teeth to bite back a scream of much-needed emotional release. Her wrath continued until the door to her room closed behind her, shutting out the sound of Cort's amusement.

Then a wave of pure despair engulfed her, as ego-bruising as the loss of her first golf competition at the tender age of ten. Throwing herself across the king-size bed, she buried her face in the softness of the white spread and gave in to the commonly used womanly reaction to heartache. She cried. Whenever she was suffering, regardless of the cause, the one infinitely effective procedure for immediate relief was always the same.

She cried hard, silent sobs, flaying the mattress with feet and fists. She cried with abandon, without analyzing the reasons for her behavior, until the hurt subsided into hiccupping sniffs.

At the same time Charlie became aware of the tear-soaked spread under her face, she heard the click of a woman's heels in the hallway approaching the room. Quickly, she pushed herself up with her arms to inspect the damage. The spread was a mess, very possibly ruined for good. *She* was a mess. She was *in* a mess. If she allowed Marita Granado into the room, she would have to provide an explanation for her breakdown. It would get back to her father, and eventually to Cort.

Lying back on the bed, and using her arms to help cover her face and the wet area of the spread, Charlie assumed an attitude of totally relaxed slumber. Mentally she controlled the residual shudders from her crying jag, and took long, deep breaths.

She heard the soft knock at the door. She heard the door open, and felt the presence of another person in the room. She heard a low, contralto voice say, "Charlie, dear, are you asleep?" She heard the soft click as the door closed again. She waited without moving.

Straining her ears, and holding her breath, to enhance her sense of hearing, she listened to the voices outside the door.

"Isn't Charlie in there, Marita?" Her father's voice sounded concerned.

"Yes, but she's asleep, Jim. The poor darling must be exhausted. I'm so glad you brought her with you. This is the perfect place for her to rest and make decisions."

Charlie's eyes clicked open and rolled toward the ceiling. That was the overstatement of the year! What she wouldn't give to provide them with a detailed description of exactly what she thought of Las Hadas and its precious ruler! But the enormous pleasure from such a recounting would be short-lived when she read the shock and incredulous expressions on their faces.

Marita and Jim would think she had lost her mind, and, perhaps they were right. What streak of idiocy had caused her to say all those unkind, unfair, and childish things to Cort? He had a right to laugh at her performance, because that's exactly what it had been!

She was so ashamed. How could she be a witness to others of the joy in walking close to God, when she allowed the devil full use of her tongue? And how could she explain her irresponsible behavior? Her desire for Cort had been so quick and so intense that, for a moment, she had felt willing to go to any lengths to bind him to her permanently.

Falling on her knees beside the massive bed, Charlie bowed her head over her folded hands, and sought answers to her troubled questions. If it was wrong to want the fulfilling love of another human being outside of marriage, why had God made her so very weak-willed? Why had He made it so difficult to be a Christian in thought and deed, as well as in name?

Dear loving, heavenly Parent ... I must be a constant disappointment to You. I'm always making promises about the wonderful things I'm going to do in Your name if You will only show me the way, and then I completely ignore Your help and guidance, and blunder on by myself. Why You haven't given up on me by now I'll never know. Be patient with me awhile longer. The older I become, the more I realize I don't fully understand about Your plans for my life. I know I love You. I know I want to be a faithful and effective witness to others of Your love. I know I'm not very good at it. I have the worst temper, Lord! My tongue absolutely runs away with me. And every time someone even hints that I might have a flaw, my pride elevates sky-high, and I defend myself with a barrage of accusations. I hope You have a great many blessings left today, because I need all You can give me. Grant me a deeper faith, and a willingness to follow the workings of your Spirit in my life.

One more thing, Lord. . . . I've always claimed to believe that "all things work together for good to them that love God" . . . and I do, so I believe that his unhappy experience with Cort will benefit me in some way. Must the workings of God be so mysterious that it can't be immediately revealed to me? Father, I don't honestly think I can stay here any longer. I need help desperately in dealing with this overpowering feeling I have for Cort! Most of all, Lord, help me guard my tongue when I'm in his presence. Drill into my mind the wisdom from Your Word: "A soft answer turneth away wrath." I don't want Cort to be angry with me any more.

CHAPTER 4

K<small>NOWING</small> SHE HAD ENGINEERED A REPRIEVE from unwanted company for at least two hours, Charlie put aside any further analysis of her feelings and set about repairing the damage her tears had made to the bedspread.

Rummaging through her still-unpacked suitcase, she located her hairdryer and plugged it into the wall socket closest to the bed. Then, sitting on the edge of the extra wide mattress, she leaned across it to direct the heat over the wet area. It took some time for the thoroughly saturated spot to dry, and, while she watched the circle gradually grow smaller, her thoughts were free to roam.

It made no sense to conclude that her deluge of tears had been in response to Cortez Ruillon's misjudgment of her, and his clearly expressed dislike. Although she couldn't recall ever having had an enemy, she was mature enough to know it was possible. What hurt most was knowing how unnecessary it was. Cort believed she was out to destroy Marita's interest in her father. He should know by now that she wasn't.

Instinctively she knew it wouldn't make a difference. Cort disliked her, period. The feelings were mutual. For the first time in her life, she actively disliked someone else. That's why she was depressed. It was against her nature to feel such intense aversion toward another human being. Any attraction she felt toward Cort was a physical one only, and she'd get over it eventually, but it bothered her greatly that she should harbor any ill feelings for him.

Rising from the bed, Charlie turned off the hair dryer and stepped back to inspect the spread from a distance. There was no indication of its saline bath.

Lethargically she unplugged the cord, wrapped it around the travel-sized appliance, and placed it on the bed. She should unpack an outfit for dinner and repair the damage to her face. Her eyes felt swollen, and were probably bloodshot. The last thing she needed now was to arouse her father's suspicions. He would never let her leave Las Hadas if he suspected the intense state of her unhappiness.

She should also decide her new destination. He'd want to know where she'd be, not to mention why she was leaving so soon after arriving. There had never been cause to deceive him before, and it made her sad to think it was necessary now. Perhaps it wasn't. She had asked God to work on her problem. She would simply have to be more trusting.

Charlie paced the cool white room. Nothing had gone right from the time she had made her announcement of the professional hiatus. She should be ecstatic, savoring her freedom and looking forward to a year of relaxation and positive introspection. But here she was, essentially homeless, and without a single friend who truly cared. She was no longer free to discuss her predicament with even her beloved father.

It was Cortez Ruillon's fault.

Charlie stopped to lean against the window casing,

and peered out over a view of deep aquamarine waves rolling endlessly against pristine white sand as soft as baby powder. Unbidden, fresh tears flooded her eyes and spilled down her cheeks. Hastily she wiped them away.

She would have enjoyed two weeks at Las Hadas. The beauty and other-worldliness of the complex were indeed peaceful, making it a perfect hideaway for resting and thinking.

But, Cortez didn't want her here, and wouldn't pretend polite hospitality for the sake of an old friend's daughter for even two short weeks. Of course, he probably believed she had moved in for good. How better to keep an eagle eye on her dear father!

Cortez, Cortez, Cortez, always Cortez. She had never spent so much time thinking about one person, and he clearly wasn't a man she should be spending any time thinking about at all. She didn't even know if he was a Christian, although she couldn't help believing his behavior was not indicative of it.

Who was she trying to kid? The more she found fault, the more her body remembered its response to his forceful caresses and kisses. Like a shameful wanton, it had— *she had*—abandoned all shreds of common decency, and not only reacted positively, but practically begged for more.

It was demoralizing. Cort said he had changed his mind about her. At first he thought she was too immature to leave her father's home, now he probably equated her with a bar-room hussy. He found the entire episode humorous. Never, never would she forget the sound of his laughter.

Charlie stripped off her blouse and slacks and threw them onto the bed, marching staunchly into the bathroom to turn on the shower spigots. She had made the right decision. She had to leave tomorrow. Another day at Las Hadas would be dangerous. She would not be used for a doormat by anyone, and that included Cortez, but he could succeed in making her one if she stayed in her present state of mind.

Pausing in front of the vanity mirror, Charlie caught a glimpse of herself. In spite of the red-rimmed eyes, her face was flushed with a strange glow. She looked different, more . . . feminine, less . . . sporty. She leaned forward to study her features close up. Her wide-set eyes were still the same violet-blue, but they appeared older, wiser, more expectant. Her small, straight nose, flecked with a few scattered freckles from the sun, was the same. Her overly generous mouth was not. It looked fuller, pinker, riper.

Embarrassed with her imaginative assessment, Charlie touched her lips with tentative fingers and remembered the hard pressure of male lips intent on punishing. They had succeeded in arousing her entire body to fever pitch.

Just before steam from the shower covered the mirror, erasing her image, Charlie saw what only the remembrance of Cort's kiss did to her face and body. Her active imagination provided a different picture of how she had actually appeared to Cort while protesting her enjoyment of it. Quickly, she stepped under the hot shower, and let the penalizing force of the water-massage drum out the image from her mind.

An hour later, Charlie stood in front of the mirror once more. This time, she was fully dressed in a lavender silk shirt and matching slacks. The color deepened the intensity of her eyes and gave them greater importance. She had carefully covered any signs of redness with make-up, and opted against wearing a dress. She was more comfortable in pants, and comfort was important tonight.

For her father's sake, however, she compromised with her determination to appear plain, and wore a couple gold rings and bracelets. A large gold puffed heart, a gift from him, hung from a fine chain around her neck.

Making a silent prayer for divine support in remembering she was her own woman, and entitled to make spur of the moment decisions, Charlie walked with swinging strides down to the wide marble entry of the villa. There, a smiling house-boy motioned for her to follow him. He led her down another long, expansive passage equal to its counterpart upstairs, and she murmured a polite, *"Gracias,"* when he paused at the entrance to an enormous living room.

Stopping inside the room, Charlie gave Cort high marks for the stunning results of his sense of design. Gleaming white surfaces, from floor to ceiling, receded in importance as they made the outdoors and the people inside the center of interest. An unrestrained 180-degree view of nature's extravagant beauty was provided through a multitude of immense windows and sliding glass doors. Again, Cort kept the use of indoor color to a minimum. Paintings, throw pillows, and vases of fresh flowers gave the striking setting warmth and homeliness, two essential ingredients for relaxed conversation and comfort.

"Charlie!" A quick flash of magenta swept into the room from the terrace. "I was on my way up to see whether you had awakened from your little nap. Our men returned from their inspection tour a few minutes ago, and will join us shortly. Do you feel a bit more rested? I was delighted to see you had succumbed to our slower pace with such ease." Marita Granado's spontaneous congeniality put Charlie in a better mood.

"You might be delighted, Marita, but I am shocked by my behavior. It was totally unlike me. I'm sorry we missed our private get-together." Charlie was equally amazed at how easily the deceptive words came to her. They weren't an all-out lie, but she knew they referred to her emotional breakdown, and not to a nap. She justified her explanation with a reminder that it would be worse to speak ill of Marita's brother and possibly ruin the relationship between them in the future.

"No matter. We'll have all day tomorrow. I don't believe Jim can be persuaded to take even one full day of respite from work, do you?"

"No," laughed Charlie in agreement. "He's too excited about his new project. I suspect it's rather like finally receiving the long-wished-for electric train he never had as a boy. This golden opportunity is his new toy, and one he won't tire of soon."

Marita chuckled. "You have such a colorful way of putting things. Men do tend to treat a job like a game sometimes, don't they? And for men like Jim and Cortez, the more challenging, unique, and rewarding the game . . . the harder they go at it."

Marita sobbered, and her warm brown eyes skimmed Charlie's face before concentrating on the massive bouquet of golden yellow hybrid hibiscus decorating the table beside them. Her delicate hands fussed with the arrangement, pretending to improve the placement of each stalk of blooms. "Do you mind, Charlie?"

"Not one bit, Marita." It didn't take a genius to understand the real meaning behind her hesitant question. "Dad and I are very close, but we've never interfered with each other's private life . . . at least, not on purpose. We do what we want to do. Until now, we've been able to be together a great deal, but we don't need to be."

"Then you won't mind that it will take a year or more of his time to design and build the course for Las Hadas?"

Charlie met Marita's look with steady eyes. "I don't mind," she repeated. "I'm thrilled he has been given the opportunity, and delighted he has accepted the challenge. My only concern is for his happiness.

He must succeed in designing a golf course which measures up to his dreams, or he won't *be* happy, though. The acclaim of other professional course architects will be important to him. He can't afford to get side-tracked by other concerns. That's why . . ."

Hearing a sound behind her, Charlie turned her head. Cort Ruillon leaned indolently against a post forming part of the arched entrance. His dark eyes never left her face. "Go on, Charlie," he drawled, "that's why, what?"

His presence in the room was enough to put her on edge, but the insinuation in his question halted her planned response. She had intended to say, that's why she would leave Las Hadas tomorrow. She didn't want her father to feel responsible for her happiness, or concern himself with undue worry about her future plans anymore. Cort obviously thought she was warning Marita against involvement with Jim. Again.

"Hello, Cort," Charlie greeted him, ignoring his question entirely. "When did you arrive?"

His lips formed a half smile. "I believe I came in on, 'or he won't be happy.' "

"Shame on you, Cort!" Marita chastised, walking over to tuck her hand under his arm. "Eavesdropping on girl-talk is wicked. You should have let us know you were here."

"I didn't want to interrupt you, my dear. It sounded like heavy stuff." His gaze flashed to Charlie, and her stomach fluttered with a dozen butterflies.

"We were merely discussing Jim's enthusiasm over the new project, brother-of-mine. Now that you're here, you can make us each a tall, cool fruit drink. Charlie and I insist on your undivided attention tonight. It is difficult for us to compete with your business pursuits. After tomorrow, we'll have to take a back seat for a while."

Cort threw back his head and laughed heartily, his dark eyes dancing. "Marita, darling, I can read you like a book. You're fishing for another compliment. I'll be glad to oblige you, but it would be coming from the wrong man." He held her at arm's length, and teased her with a critical perusal. "Mmm, you'll do, for one so old."

Marita pushed him away, slanting a petulant look in his direction. "You rascal! See if I ever help you out of a jam again. Even Alejandro knows the Golden Rule!"

Charlie observed their friendly banter with a stirring of jealousy mixed with pain. If her own brother were still alive, she'd have someone else to care for her, as Cort so obviously cared for Marita. Cort had every right to laugh over her ridiculous accusation earlier. He would certainly provide for a member of his family, and consider it a privilege.

"Charlie, help me out. Cort has succeeded in completely deflating my ego. I've been in mothballs so long, I don't trust my own judgment any more. Do I really look . . . old?"

Charlie smiled over Marita's sudden insecurity. "About as old as a college cheerleader. With your flawless skin and high cheekbones, you could still be a photographer's model, if you chose. You're more than physically beautiful, Marita. Your inner love-liness makes everyone around you feel better . . . younger. That's more important. By the way," she added, "your lovely dress couldn't be more perfect for you."

"Oh, my dear," choked Marita. She caught a shimmering tear at the edge of each widened eye with the tip of an index finger, capped with a glossy pink nail. "You're too kind, but I thank you, Charlie." She blinked away the moisture from her lashes, and reached up to plant a kiss on Charlie's cheek.

"Are you ready for those refreshments, or not?" Cort's question was faintly tinged with sarcasm. He glowered at them and ran an impatient hand through his thick ebony hair.

"Yes, of course we are, Cort, but you needn't growl at us like some old bear. If you had paid proper court, as a well-bred *caballero* should, we wouldn't need to seek reassurance from each other. Poor Charlie, I don't believe you've spoken more than two words to her. I'm surprised at you. You're usually not reticent in your appreciation of beauty." Marita put her arm around Charlie's waist and propelled her toward the veranda in Cort's wake.

Swift color flooded Charlie's face. "You can't appreciate what isn't there, Marita. I'm not known on the tour as a sex symbol, like Jan Stephenson, or a stunning beauty, like Laura Baugh. I'm afraid my fans and business managers project a well-scrubbed, all-American look for me . . . hardly Cort's type."

While she spoke, Charlie eyed her host with uninhibited interest, grateful for the opportunity to do so without his knowledge. He led the way across the living room and out onto the spacious patio, furnished with an abundance of white wrought-iron lounges and chairs. Reluctantly, she admitted to herself, he was definitely *her* type.

Since she was fairly tall herself, Cort's domineering height, with broad shoulders tapering to narrow muscular hips and thighs, were infinitely attractive to her. He was a study in color contrasts when compared to the majority of the fair-complexioned men she knew.

They had reached the seating group, and Marita sank onto the comfort of a lounge plumped with pale canvas-covered cushions. Cort busied himself at another portable beverage cart, laden with several clear crystal decanters of freshly prepared fruit juices so popular throughout Mexico—pineapple, mango, papaya, lime, and orange.

Finding herself irritated by his lack of response to her casual put-down, Charlie walked to the edge of the patio and leaned with her forearms against a low encompassing wall. At dusk, the sea and sky presented a constantly changing canvas. For a few seconds her attention was diverted.

"I have always thought that any women who dressed in sport togs had a clean-cut image. I can't imagine otherwise!" Marita exclaimed suddenly.

"Unless she wore a polo shirt one size too small and kept the buttons unfastened."

Anger flashed through Charlie with licking red heat, and she struggled for self-control before whirling to confront Cort. His gaze met hers easily, in a face completely devoid of expression. "I'm surprised to hear a comment like that from you, Cort, even in jest. As a former member of the PGA, you know that golf is a sport dependent on its rules. Most professionals honor them without argument, and that goes for the administrative rules of the organization as well. The LPGA supports individuality, but not the kind which detracts from the seriousness of the competition. Most of us women on the tour like to look good; *feminine* , if you will, *not sexy*. Nice looking pros bring out large galleries, and that means more money and better press coverage. But, we're intelligent enough to know it takes unadultrated concentration on our game to keep up their fickle interest and to be a winner . . . a consistent winner; and, in case you aren't aware of it, *I am a winner*. I follow the rules."

Charlie's voice had risen in intensity, but it was still restrained, considering the depth of her agitation. Her frosty pale violet eyes glinted with a non-stop barrage of icicles hurled in Cort's direction.

"Bravo!" applauded Marita, casting a quick glance in her brother's direction. "Cort isn't accustomed to a women with a strong sense of herself, Charlie. Perhaps that's why he's hesitant to express his appreciation of your enviable beauty. Come now, Cort. Confess. Charlie might exude a look of naïveté and fresh, wide-eyed innocence out of the fairways, but right now, she is undeniably more appealing."

"You're absolutely right, Marita. Miss Summers is lonely, and I'm beginning to appreciate her other . . . unique qualities . . . more and more, the better I get to know her." Cort moved forward to present their drinks with panther strides, the lines of his muscled thighs pushing against the fabric of his summer-weight dress slacks.

He handed a tall iced glass topped with lime to Charlie, and startled her by keeping his fingers on it until she looked up. The teasing glint in his enigmatic eyes dared her to make an issue of the double entendre in his words.

The struggle to keep from taking the glass and hurling its contents into his face was difficult, but she had vowed to match wits with Cort and not let him get the best of her.

"Thank you, Cort," she murmured politely, with downcast eyes. "You don't really know anything about my qualities, you know," she added, for his hearing only. She applied gentle pressure to wrest the drink from his grasp, but his strong lean fingers didn't budge.

"I know you're insecure about your femininity," he whispered back. Amusement twitched the corners of his mouth. "That didn't take long to find out."

Charlie closed her eyes against the pain his words inflicted. She didn't want to be reminded of her reaction to his kiss. Slowly she removed her hand from the glass, and stepped backward in order to meet his gaze. "You don't know me at all," she protested softly, "and you never will, because you're too callous and intolerant to see beyond your nose."

"I see a great deal more than you're giving me credit for, I think. Did you know that hate is very closely akin to love, Charlie? Think about it. You're overreacting to me again." He moved away to hand Marita a frosty glass before Charlie could think of a reply, and she was relieved that his sister had been

70

too preoccupied to pay attention to their conversation.

Reverting to her perusal of the sea, Charlie fought to keep her emotional turmoil from becoming apparent. Why was Cort so intent on upsetting her? It wasn't at all in character with the man for whom her father had such deep admiration. Something about her was causing him to behave differently toward her. Did she remind him of his former wife? Was he retaliating for her earlier hurtful accusations? Or, heaven forbid, was her judgment of him indeed exaggerated?

"Good evening, everyone. I guess I'm the last one here." Jim Summers' voice preceded him across the patio.

"Last, perhaps, but not least, Jim. Come keep me company. I was beginning to feel in the way. Cort and Charlie are ignoring me, for some reason." Marita laughed becomingly, and held out her hand to him.

"I'm sure you're stretching the truth a bit, Marita. As I said before, you're quite impossible to ignore." He took her hand, and bent to lightly touch the slender fingers with his lips. "You're an irresistible splash of color in this sea of white, my dear."

"What can I fix you to drink from this assortment of juices, Jim?" Cort interrupted the intimacy of their conversation.

"Whatever you're serving the others is fine, Cort."

"Hello, Dad." Strolling to her father's side, Charlie put her arm around his waist and reached up to kiss him. "Can you believe we're actually here? It doesn't seem right that we're so far away from home and not preparing for a tournament tomorrow."

He kissed her in return, and squeezed her shoulder affectionately. "You know what they say, honey girl. You're never too old to change."

"I thought *they* said you can't teach an old dog new tricks."

"Hmm, contradictions, aren't they? Perhaps the

71

secret is to exclude myself from both on the pretext I'm not old. What do you think?''

"I think you're finally thinking right." Charlie avoided her father's searching gaze by taking a long drink of the frosty concoction in her glass. The tang of lime clung to her lips, and she licked them thoughtfully while chiding herself. If she weren't careful, she would betray her unhappiness.

There was considerable laughter and continued light-hearted conversation for the next hour. Everyone was enthusiastic about the magnificent sunset, the first Charlie had observed in its entirety since she was a very young girl. Mesmerized by the kaleidoscope of ever-changing colors, she took tiny sips of her refreshing punch.

When the giant orange sun was still visible on the horizon, bathing the sea beneath it with golden ribbons, her ruminations were filled with storm clouds, though. They charged across her mind in a raging stampede, colliding and merging into a full-fledged tempest.

But with the final ray of light consumed by the greedy sea, she felt strangely at peace. Cort wasn't really her enemy; rather, her ally. *She* had made the decision to break the close tie with her father. Cort believed it was necessary. She should be grateful to him for reinforcing her conviction, not fighting him, however troublesome his methods of expression.

Charlie had chosen to stay in the background, participating in the friendly repartee on the patio only when someone spoke to her. Her eyes had been riveted on the setting sun; her mind, turned to her inner tumult. Now she turned with interest to watch her father, and to witness his undisguised contentment in being with the Ruillons.

She smiled at him when he noticed her eyes focused on his, and reached out to cover her hand as it lay on the chair arm.

"Happy, Dad?"

"As a clam," he returned. "How about you?"

Not trusting her voice, she nodded. Of their own volition, Charlie's eyes sought the face of Cort Ruillon. As she expected he was watching her, his gaze direct and uncompromising. Feeling magnanimous, she drew up the corners of her mouth in a brief, but friendly, semblance of a smile.

A muscle twitched near the corner of his jaw, but he made no attempt to return her overture of amity. Was there any softness in him at all? She searched his face for even a beginning flicker of responding warmth, but his expression was inscrutable.

What did it matter? She wasn't trying to win a personality contest. It wasn't important whether Cort liked her or not. He was distrustful of her intentions. She could understand that. When, with the passage of time, he discovered his mistake, he would apologize. She was a patient and forgiving person. If, for some reason, that day never arrived, it didn't matter. It simply didn't matter at all.

Liar. Why was she trying so hard to deceive herself?

Concealing a sigh, Charlie rested her head against the high-backed lounge and sought familiar constellations in the prodigious number of stars overhead.

If she cared so little about Cort's approval, why did she feel empty and aching inside? If she didn't like him, why did she have such an inexorable interest in what he was doing, saying, and thinking? Why was her heartbeat increasing in speed even now?

Her eyes located Polaris, the North Star, and traced the outline of the Little Dipper. She chewed on the inside of her bottom lip and laughed silently and mirthlessly. If she were under oath in a court of law, she would plead the Fifth Amendment to questions like those. Besides, it was an exercise in futility. Whatever answers she came up with would make no difference in the weird relationship she had with Cort Ruillon.

Utter silence enveloped the spacious patio now. All of them were deeply touched by the beauty of the sunset. Suddenly Marita leaped from her lounge chair. "I'll be right back," she said. "Don't anyone move a muscle."

In less than a minute she returned with a guitar which she deposited on her brother's lap. "Sing for us, darling. It has been far too long since I've heard your voice. It's time you returned to the special things which once gave you so much pleasure."

Cort pushed the instrument away, a scowl scoring deep ridges in his forehead. "No, Marita. You know how I feel."

"I know how you *once* felt," she returned, a hint of tragedy in her voice. "At the time I sympathized with you, but now you need to get on with your life. We both do. Sing 'Day Is Dying In The West.' Tonight's beautiful sunset demands it." Marita returned to her place beside Jim and smiled up at him. He reached for her hand.

Charlie watched Cort surreptitiously from under her lashes. His head was turned toward the sea-sky, and his thoughts were miles away. Almost without conscious thought, his fingers moved, strumming one intricate chord, and then another. At first Charlie was sure the sound of the music startled him, but with each successive chord, a transformation took place. Although he seemed to be oblivious to his hushed and attentive audience, he did appear to be playing for someone else. His dark, luminous eyes stared out across the gentle waves of the quiet sea, his strong profile backed by fire-rimmed clouds.

The throbbing of sounds from the instrument in Cort's hands was filled with soul-stirring solemnity, and the sheer force of feeling being transmitted caused a great emotional turbulence within Charlie's mind.

Was he playing to his wife and child? Had they shared evenings like this before their untimely deaths? If so, she could easily understand why Cort preferred not to call up the haunting memories.

When the deep baritone voice rose from his throat and burst forth in reverent song, Charlie instinctively turned toward the sea to enjoy the last glorious view of the painted sky. Deeply touched by the tender passion in the words of the song, and in the sound of Cort's magnificent voice interpreting them, she became visibly moved. Cort Ruillon loved God as she did! She was sure of it. No one could sing with such depth without His inspiration.

> Day is dying in the west;
> Heaven is touching earth with rest;
> Wait and worship while the night
> Sets her evening lamps alight
> Through all the sky.
>
> While the deepening shadows fall,
> Heart of Love, enfolding all,
> Through the glory and the grace
> Of the stars that veil Thy face,
> Our hearts ascend.
>
> When forever from our sight
> Pass the stars, the day, the night,
> Lord of angels, on our eyes
> Let eternal morning rise,
> And shadows end.

With Cort's voice ringing in glorious harmony with the pleading strains of the guitar chords, Charlie turned to fill her eyes with the sight of him, her heart pounding wildly.

> Holy, holy, holy
> Lord God of Hosts!
> Heav'n and earth are full of Thee!
> Heav'n and earth are praising Thee,
> O Lord Most High.

The rendering was almost a benediction and, for several minutes, no one moved or spoke. Then Cort himself made the first attempt to shake off the moving seriousness of the moment. He placed the guitar on the patio against the encompassing wall and turned to smile at his sister, a silent understanding passing between them.

Charlie shivered again. Whenever she witnessed such a smile from the face of Cortez Ruillon, she doubted her discernment. What kind of man was this, who could move heaven and earth with his very being?

"Come, everyone." Marita rose from her chair and stretched imaginary kinks from her back. "Carlos has given the word. It's time to feed our bodies. Our souls have received all the sustenance they're going to get from the elements tonight."

She smiled into Jim's appreciative cerulean eyes, and reached out to haul him from his adjoining seat. "Come, *Señor* Summers, you have the honor of escorting me to the dining room."

"An honor which I accept with great pleasure, *señora.*"

Charlie watched them walk across the veranda and into the softly lighted living room. They were completely oblivious to her presence. Did her father know that Marita was in love with him? Did he welcome her affection with intentions of returning it? Had he already made up his mind before accepting Cort's job offer, or had he accepted it in order to clarify his feelings for Marita?

"Are you planning to sit there all night? Like it or not, Charlie, you're my dinner partner, and I'm famished. Let's go."

Cort's command rankled, and Charlie went rigid before facing him, her eyes widened in indignation. "Didn't you ever learn to say *please?* " She made no attempt to move from the chair.

"Does our every conversation have to be a sparring match?" he countered, sighing in exasperation.

"We've never *had* a real conversation, so I can't answer your question. You have threatened me and warned me. You have ordered me and accused me. You have criticized me. You have never *attempted* to *converse* with me."

"Oh, for sweet pity's sake! It's impossible to have a conversation with you!" Cort paced in front of her. "You jump down my throat the second I speak a word to you."

Charlie leaped to her feet. "Isn't it rather odd that no one else has that difficulty?" Her voice rose one decibel in volume.

Cort stopped in front of her. "What's odd is why you insist on baiting, goading, and arguing with me. You misinterpret everything I say!"

"I do no such thing! I merely refuse to be treated like a child."

"Then, stop acting like one!"

"Stop acting like . . ." Charlie's hands were tight fists against her sides. "You're *insufferable!* You started all this commotion because of your boorish manners. I simply reminded you of the magic word, *please.* It's amazing how well it works. It has the power to turn an order into a request. Most people respond positively to requests. I do." She glared at Cort, her blood boiling. "Now, if you will *please* excuse me, I'd like to join my father for dinner, although I'm almost afraid to eat. My portion will probably be poisoned." She didn't wait for a response, but spun with an insolent flip of her long fair hair.

"Wait, Charlie!" Cort snapped, his eyes glinting like diamonds. "Please . . ."

Her cheeks on fire, Charlie stood there staring into his smoldering eyes. "All right," she said, sighing consent. "I'm waiting."

"I would appreciate it if you could try to hide your contempt for me during dinner." He stayed her retort with a gesture. "For your father's sake, and Marita's as well. I'd like Jim's first evening at Las Hadas to be a pleasant one, and yours, too. I'm not the complete ogre you seem to find me. I have an excellent cook. Your food will not be poisoned, but it can't possibly be enjoyed in anger. Perhaps we could start over?"

For a fleeting moment, Charlie was tempted to refuse. But, when his features relaxed, and the corner of his mouth twitched with the suggestion of a smile, she was lost.

"Sure," she said blandly, pretending a nonchalance she didn't feel. "Why not? I'm willing, if you are."

"Thank you, Charlie. I appreciate your coopera-tion." His voice was edged with amusement, and she fidgeted nervously with the heavy bracelets on her wrist. "Perhaps you would take my arm, then, and we could appear to be great friends when we enter the dining room."

Charlie's color deepened and she threw him a measured glance.

"Please."

The word was spoken so softly she scarcely heard it. Was he playing games with her? Or had her words gotten through to him? Was he sincerely trying to apologize and make amends? She couldn't afford to thumb her nose at his gesture of appeasement—not if they might be related through marriage some day. She wouldn't like to be responsible for bringing Marita and her father heartache.

"I can act as well as you, Cort," she said lightly. "Between the two of us, we should be able to convince two unsuspecting people that all is well in Camelot." She held out her arm. "Lead on, Your Highness."

Cort's mouth opened, as though to say something, and closed when he changed his mind.

It was a long quiet trip to the dining room. Charlie had the distinct feeling she was on her way to the guillotine, and if Cort had his way, it would be her head placed on the chopping block. She wasn't allowing God much opportunity to control of her life . . . let alone her tongue.

Don't abandon me now! she prayed earnestly, trying not to tremble with the thrill of Cort's hard muscular arm entwined with hers. *How can I ever ask him about his relationship with You when I continue to sound like an old shrew? He'll never believe the real reason for my career hiatus if I can't become a more visibly effective witness of Your saving grace. Forgive me for failing You so often, Lord, and please give me a double dose of Christian patience and charity. At least enough to get through this evening!*

CHAPTER 5

MUCH TO CHARLIE'S SURPRISE, the next two hours passed quickly and enjoyably. Conversation drifted amiably from one noncontroversial topic to another, and ranged from a discussion of Mexico's discovery of oil to the effects of high interest rates on the American economy. The men voiced their disgust with baseball and football strikes during the playing season, and Marita encouraged Charlie to talk about her career in professional golf.

"I'm ashamed to say that other than hearing the final announcement on television sportcasts of the latest winner of a specific tournament, I know practically nothing about women's golf," Marita apologized.

"It isn't your fault. Unfortunately, we're given very little attention by reporters, and those following us on the circuit ask the same old questions about birdies and bogeys and final scores. It makes for boring news reports." Charlie leaned forward eagerly. Here was a topic she could enthusiastically discuss.

"Golf drama doesn't televise very well at all. The

action unfolds too slowly. Spectators should walk the course with the pros in order to feel the power and tension, and witness the courage and strategy the players must use. Every minute they're out there, they do constant battle with themselves, the elements, and their competitors. Every course is vastly different, you know, and every lie of the ball challenges their abilities to choose the right club and the proper swing, and to get it into the best possible position for the next shot at the hole." Charlie smiled at Marita. "Competition on the professional tour is . . . quite demanding."

"Is that why you quit?"

Cort's unexpected question caught Charlie off guard. She placed the dessert fork on her plate with deliberate precision.

"She didn't quit, Cort," inserted Jim, after a hasty glance at Charlie's face. "She's just taking a little vacation. In eight years of professional competition, she hasn't had a break. You must remember how fierce it can be out there. When every stroke you make means money, and more money means bigger business, the pressure can be mind-boggling."

"Of course it can," soothed Marita. "Especially when you're a champion, and have so many people depending on your continued success. I don't know how you've kept it up so long, Charlie."

Casting a quick look of thanks at her father and Marita, Charlie sat back in her chair and folded her hands in front of her on the table. She contemplated her blunt-cut, highly buffed nails before answering. "The late Vince Lombardi once said, 'Winning isn't everything, it's the only thing!' It took great patience on Dad's part to make me realize this didn't mean I had to win at all costs every time I played. It meant I had to prepare myself physically and mentally to win in every game, to do my best, but *then* to be content with the results of that game. I do this by taking my practice sessions seriously, and by concentrating only on my very next shot. I don't bemoan my previous one, or concern myself with what my partner is doing. By playing each stroke as it comes, I save myself a great deal of emotional wear and tear."

Marita sighed. "Suddenly, the sport doesn't seem as glamorous as I thought when following Cort around the fairways. Of course, that was several years ago."

"I thought pro golf was glamorous, too, when I first joined the tour. I had grown up following famous personalities around the courses in Palm Springs. Most of the greats in golf played there. I watched Arnie Palmer, Jack Nicklaus, Marilyn Smith, Kathy Whitworth and Mickey Wright. I got autographs from Dinah Shore, Bob Hope and Bing Crosby. When you see the winners of major tournaments receiving fancy cars and elaborate trophies, and witness the adulation given them by the fans and press, it's very difficult to anticipate the negative side."

"Now that you mention it, I can remember Cort's running on only nervous energy at times. Don't you recall how much Helena complained of how the pressure was ruining your health, Cort?" Instantly she pressed her fingers over her lips as if regretting the reminder.

Charlie threw him a sharp glance, noticing the strain on his hardened features, and took a hasty sip of her water. She realized that she, too, had been thoughtlessly cruel when using references to his dead wife in order to defend herself from strongly voiced disapproval.

Jim broke the thick silence. "What do you ladies plan to do with yourselves tomorrow? I'm eager to hear about it because it will be a day to remember for Charlie. Believe it or not, she actually left her golf clubs at home, and has vowed only to read, swim, and sleep for two weeks."

"Good for her," said Marita. "Then that's exactly what we'll do." She patted her lips with her napkin.

"Actually, Dad, I've been meaning to talk to you about that." Charlie took a deep breath. Here it was—time for her most convincing performance. "As soon as we got on the plane, I was regretting my decision. You know me all too well. I'm simply not happy unless I play at least one round a day. By the time we reached Las Hadas this afternoon, and I saw how beautiful Mexico was, I became itchy to see more of it. Since then, I've . . . come up with a brilliant plan. I'm going to fly back home tomorrow, pick up my clubs, and then play all the courses I've read about that aren't on the tour. I can spend afternoons and evenings sightseeing. I'll start out at the Princess Hotel in Acapulco. I might even fly down to Rio and Lima. When will I ever get the opportunity to do this again? I'm going to take copious notes, and write a bestseller on my adventure!"

Charlie was breathless by the time she had finished her presentation, and hoped her eyes weren't overly bright, or her cheeks too rouged by her guilt. The look on her father's face made her throat constrict, but she forced herself to feign even more excitement. "Well?" she encouraged. "What do you think? Bet you thought it would take me months to decide what to do with my hiatus, and it has taken only a few days. I can't wait to get started!"

"Charlie . . ." Jim began, clearing his throat.

"You haven't been here an entire day yet, Charlie," Marita interrupted. "I won't let you go! Not so soon. I've looked forward to meeting you for years. Convince her, Cort. Tell her she must stay for at least two weeks. You know how badly Alejandro will feel if she leaves tomorrow."

"I'll visit with him awhile after dinner, Marita," Charlie continued. Why must they make it so difficult for her? "We have the rest of the evening to spend together. Really, I must go tomorrow. The longer I stay here, the lazier I'll become. I wasn't thinking straight before. If I don't play golf every day, I'll lose the calluses on my hands, and that will change my swing. You know how important my grip is, Dad.'' She was chattering like a lunatic. Her dad would see through her act like a homing pigeon zeroing in on its target through a fog. Likewise, Cort. He must know her plans were a direct result of his threats and warnings.

"Your grip is important, but a couple weeks shouldn't matter, Charlie. You won't be playing tournament golf for a while. You'll have plenty of time to regain what little you'd lose. I'm sure Cort could locate a set of clubs like yours to use while you're here.'' Jim appealed to her with his eyes and his words.

"But there isn't a course to play on," Charlie protested. Her eyes fell before his. It hurt too much to watch him while she continued to fib.

"Cort has an excellent short, par-3 course. You could work on your chip shots and putting. You don't have any problems with your drives or fairway irons, anyway.''

"But . . ." Charlie faltered.

"Cort, make her stay," Marita begged.

"Stop it, *please!*"

"*Charlie!*"

Her father's gasp of astonishment halted Charlie's rising impatience while she still had her fists on the table. Had she really shouted down their protests with such incredibly rude behavior? No wonder her dad was so shocked.

Sagging back into her chair, she cast him a remorseful look. "Sorry, everyone. I hate it when I lose my temper. I can't even blame it on jet lag," she laughed humorlessly. "I'm a little upset, I guess, because I wanted Dad to be as excited about my plans as I am. Of course I want to get to know you, Marita, but I'm sure this isn't the last opportunity we'll have. If Dad is going to spend a year here, I'll stop by to see him in a few weeks . . . if I am welcome, that is. It isn't as though you had planned on my being here, anyway. I have already disrupted your schedule with my unexpected visit.''

All this time, Cort had sat in stony silence. Angry with him for driving her into such a distasteful display of manners, Charlie glared at him defiantly.

"Charlie,'' he said, his deep, low-pitched voice barely audible, "your decision to tour Mexico does seem rather hasty. Surely it wouldn't hurt to give a few more days of thought to the plan. In the meantime, you could discuss it with your father, and Marita will be able to visit with you. Doesn't that sound reasonable?''

The *audacity* of the man! After as much as *demanding* that she leave Las Hadas, after insinuating that she had *forced* her visit on them, after telling her *repeatedly* how unwelcome she was, how *dare* he sit there and pretend her efforts to leave were only another willful, selfish, and thoughtless display of her supposed immaturity! Oh, if only they were alone, she'd tell him what she thought of him in no uncertain terms!

Charlie carefully schooled her voice to tones of friendly civility. "This isn't a decision which needs discussion with my father. He understands, as I'm sure Marita does. My decision to tour Mexico is no more hasty than was my father's to have me join him here in the first place. At one time or other, we all make hasty decisions . . . including you, no doubt.''

She threw him a puckish smile. "Often, such decisions are the right ones, the . . . best ones,'' she added pointedly. *Or are you too dense to understand this was your decision?* her look accused.

Marita reached over to place her slender hand on Charlie's, and squeezed it affectionately. "Whatever you decide, I will understand, Charlie. Cort and I don't have the right to influence you one way or the other. I was being selfish. I'll be sorry if you leave tomorrow, but look forward to hearing about your exciting travels when you return."

"Be that as it may," said Cort, pushing back his chair and rising in one fluid motion, "she can't go anywhere without a reservation on the one plane flying out of Manzanillo each day. The seats are generally booked in advance. I'll need to check on space availability. It's possible there won't be anything for a few days."

"That's right," agreed Marita with a hopeful note in her voice. "Sometimes a guest has to be put on the waiting list, Charlie. But at least we'll have most of tomorrow. The plane doesn't leave until late afternoon."

"Only one plane?" Charlie questioned, aghast.

"That's right. One plane each day, and usually completely booked in advance. I'll go to my study and call the airport right now." Cort grinned, immodestly pleased with her discomfiture.

"I'll come with you. I want to speak with the agent myself."

"Of course. Take Jim into the living room, Marita. We'll join you there when we're finished." Cort motioned to Charlie, his attitude one of amused patience. "Down the hall, and to your right."

"Lead on, Your Highness. I'll follow." She was at the end of her patience. If she had to sleep at the airport, she would. Not for anything would she stay in this prison. Not one more day!

Charlie followed Cort into his study and waited by his desk during his short conversation with the hotel operator. Since he was speaking in Spanish, she could only hope that he was following through as promised.

Replacing the telephone receiver, he advised, "You might as well be seated. We'll have to wait a few minutes."

"I'd rather stand."

"Stand then. I plan to sit. I've put in a long day." He slid onto a high-backed leather chair, and put his feet up on the corner of the desk. Then, picking up a magazine, he idly thumbed through it.

His air of righteous indifference needled Charlie. Pacing the floor, she studied the pattern on the antique Persian carpet, and when that failed to hold her attention, shifted to a blind examination of the books lining two walls. Each rustle of another turned page grated more deeply on her nerves until finally she heaved a long sigh of exasperation.

"You might as well relax, Charlie. The call will come when the connection is made. Impatience won't affect those at the other end one iota."

"Oh, be quiet!"

"My, my, such an unladylike attitude."

"I'm warning you, Cort! I've had it up to my eyebrows with you!"

"I don't understand what this is all about, Charlie. I came in here to call the airport for you. Isn't that what you wanted? You can't leave Las Hadas without a plane reservation." The inflection of his voice never fluctuated from its steady low drone.

"I'll leave with or without one, make no mistake about that! If I have to *walk,* I will leave this place tomorrow, and don't pretend that isn't exactly what you wanted me to do!" Charlie felt her temper rise with each word. "You forced me into this deception, Cort. I feel sick inside. *Sick!* Do you hear me? I've lied to my father for the first time in my life, all because of you! How can you live with yourself You actually sat in that room and maliciously implied *I* was being *unreasonable* in attempting to leave here tomorrow, when you *knew* I was . . . I was . . ."

Once the tears began, there was no stopping them. They continued to roll faster than she could wipe them away with her fingers. When her nose joined the deluge, she sniffed loudly and used the back of her hand and wrist. "I . . . hate you, Cortez R-Ruillon!"

"No you don't. I don't believe you could hate anyone." Cort was right beside her. She hadn't heard him leave his chair and cross the room. He pushed a clean handkerchief into her hand and watched her dry her eyes and blow her nose.

Before she could continue her tirade, the telephone shrilled with loud persistence. Cort answered it, carrying on a long conversation entirely in Spanish. After he replaced the receiver, he sat on the edge of the desk. "That was the airport."

"The airport!" Charlie exploded. "I said I wanted to . . ."

Cort loomed tall in front of her. "Pipe down and listen. Nothing good is ever accomplished by erupting like a volcano. . . . I have decided you should remain here as requested by your father."

"*You* decided!" Charlie sputtered.

"I've made a plane reservation for you for two weeks from today. You've upset your father. He won't be able to concentrate on his job if he has to worry about you gallivanting helter-skelter around the world on some whim."

"He won't need to worry. I'll write to him. They do deliver mail to this place, don't they?"

"Stop splitting hairs. I thought you claimed to know Jim. If you weren't so busy thinking of yourself, you'd know how he feels right now."

"If I weren't thinking of *myself*? What about *you*? People in glass houses shouldn't throw stones."

"I'm tired of all this bickering, Charlie. You won't be leaving for two weeks, so why don't you just make the best of it? Now go upstairs and repair your make-up, then we'll give your father the welcome news. I'll wait for you here."

Realizing there was no point in arguing, Charlie turned on her heels and stalked to the door of the study. Intending to slam the door behind her in one last personal statement on his dictatorial methods, she swung around to make sure she had Cort's attention.

He was standing at the window with his back to the door, his broad shoulders slightly drooped. Charlie's breath caught in her throat. His head hung forward in an attitude of extreme fatigue. He appeared older, and . . . defeated. Had his decision to have her stay at Las Hadas been an admission of guilt . . . his stubborn way of conceding without losing face? Could he himself possibly have wanted her to stay longer? Certainly he had made known his desire to please his sister and nephew . . . and her father. For the life of her, she couldn't figure him out. One minute, he was acting the arrogant dictator; the next, an unusually sad and vulnerable man, at loose ends with himself, his life, and with God.

Afraid to carry her thoughts any further, Charlie left the study door open and fled swiftly through the villa and up the sweeping marble stairway in long leggy strides. For the first time all day, a smile teased the corners of her mouth.

Was this God's answer to her prayer for redirection of her life? Had he sent her to Las Hadas . . . this sun-washed fairy tale palace . . . this place for making wishes and knowing they could very well come true? She would try harder to keep her tongue leashed, to listen more intently to the working of the Holy Spirit in her heart. She would continue to pray for answers, and, in the meantime, enjoy all Las Hadas had to offer . . . *including* the opportunity to know its owner better.

CHAPTER 6

THE NEXT MORNING Charlie rose soon after dawn and walked the cliff-rimmed private beach of the resort while the other guests were still asleep. She explored every inch of the gleaming white sand to the most remote corner, where her exit was blocked by a craggy outpost of rock. She reclined against a petrous chair carved by the passage of time and an angry sea, and stared out over the placid blue waters of the bay. Only the lapping of quiet waves against the shore and the occasional screech of a gull disturbed her idyllic dreams—the search for peace and a meaningful premise on which to base her future. Never had she prayed so hard for the guidance of the Holy Spirit; never had she felt so reassured of God's love.

When the sounds of a waking world invaded her privacy, she leaped up, jogged back to the area where attendants had carefully raked the sand free of debris beached during the night by the tide, and flung herself into the water for a vigorous morning swim.

By her second day, she found an enormous yellow towel and a body-sized vinyl cushion waiting for her on the beach, placed there by the thoughtful resort attendants who worked under one of the dozen white canvas Moorish cabanas lining the water's edge. Thankful for the unaccustomed luxury, she basked in the early morning sun until she was dry.

Once, when she sat up to feast on the bold beauty of the compound, she saw Cortez standing at the edge of the cliff on which he had built his villa. He was watching her. Disturbed, and feeling vulnerable under his dark gaze, she quickly pulled the fluffy towel over her swimsuit. When she sliced another look from the corner of her eyes, he was gone.

True to his word, Cort was rarely around during the day. At dinner in the early evenings, he involved himself in deep discussions with Jim. After dinner the two men excused themselves and retired to the study to pour over aerial and off-shore photographs of the land designated for the championship golf course.

Charlie knew they spent most of those first days using every available vehicle to study the terrain. Her father began a few preliminary sketches, but he would alter and improve them many times before allowing any work to begin outdoors.

An easy camaraderie developed between Marita and Charlie. Each of them shared liberally of childhood reminiscences, but carefully skirted any discussion of Marita's and Jim's interest in each other. Charlie felt no jealousy; rather, she enjoyed speculating on the changes an expanded family would make in Jim's life and in her own.

The first morning she had crept down the stairs to make her way to the beach, a new golf bag filled with an assortment of clubs, exactly like her own at home, was propped against the wall at the foot of the stairs. Cort had scrawled a brief note and taped it to the bag.

"Please accept the use of these during your visit. Alejandro will show you how to reach the clubhouse. The manager's name is Diego Ortiz. He has instruc-

tions to outfit you with shoes, balls, tees, and anything else you might need. Play as often as you like. Cortez. P.S. Notice, I said please."

Still smarting from Cort's highhanded methods, Charlie ignored his attempt at humor, and ignored the clubs as well. She passed them on her way back upstairs to change for breakfast, again on her way down, and again after eating. This time, Alejandro sat on the step beside them.

"Buenos dias, Charlie. Are you going to play golf now? I'll be your caddy. If you wear your hat, we'll look like partners." He flashed her a wide-toothed grin, and tugged on the brim of his bright red headgear.

"I don't think so, pal. I thought I'd sunbathe out by the pool for a while."

"But you've already been swimming, Charlie. I saw you come in from the beach before breakfast. *Tio* Cortez said I should take you to play golf this morning."

"Your uncle should have discussed my plans with me."

"He'll think I disobeyed him if you don't go."

"Alejandro, it is rude to argue with a houseguest." Marita broke into the conversation. "Apologize at once." Her voice was almost too beautiful to be taken seriously, but Alejandro heard the underlying steel and complied without a second reminder.

"Forgive me, Charlie," he muttered, all sparkle from his dark eyes dulled by disappointment. "I had hoped you would teach me how to play. Then, when the new course is complete, *Tio* Cortez would let me play with him." He slumped on the bottom stair and propped his chin on one fist.

"You know, that sounds like a good idea, Alejandro," Charlie said, touched by his forlorn expression. "I think I'd enjoy trying my hand as a teacher. You'll have to work hard, though. I won't continue giving lessons after today if you don't listen carefully and then practice faithfully."

"It isn't necessary for you to do that, Charlie. This is your vacation. Don't let Alejandro take advantage of you."

"I want to teach him, Marita. How about you? Are you a golfer? Want to come along?"

"Well, it has been many years since I tried . . ."

"Do come, Mama. Charlie can teach you, too. She's a pro, you know." Alejandro climbed two more steps and swung backward while hanging on the banister.

"Can you handle two beginners at one time, Charlie? Perhaps I'm too old to learn."

"Nonsense. Golf is a wonderful sport for people of all ages. Besides, no one is ever too old to learn. I'll give you a thirty-minute lesson each morning, and then while you practice with a particular club, I'll go off on a round of the course to sharpen my personal techniques. By next week, you should both be able to join me. It will be fun." Charlie smiled at them, hoping she sounded more confident than she felt. Teaching anyone, especially a child, took an inordinate amount of patience. To remain encouraging, without letting a note of criticism creep in to spoil a tenuous level of interest might be beyond her abilities. Young egos were tender egos.

"Wonderful!" Marita exclaimed, giving her jubilant son a warm hug. "What should I wear?"

"Anything comfortable. I usually wear an old T-shirt and a pair of shorts. You want to be free of anything which might constrict arm motion. If you don't have golf shoes, wear sneakers. I'll meet you right here in five minutes."

"Wear your baseball hat, Charlie."

Charlie yanked Alejandro's hat brim down over his face. "I couldn't golf without it, pal."

Charlie came to look forward to those hours

93

between breakfast and lunch. Both Marita and Alejandro were avid and rapid learners and seemed to have natural talent for the sport. Both had the ability to concentrate without feeling self-conscious, and that helped. Their progress brought her an amazing amount of satisfaction. She found herself doubling the amount of time spent with them, and contenting herself with only one round of nine holes practicing her own skills.

It was Charlie's idea to keep their lessons a secret from Cort and Jim because, in the back of her mind persisted the nagging threat of failure in her new role as teacher. Without knowledge of her activity, she'd be spared the memory of Cort's face stamped, once again, with ridicule and scorn. On the other hand, if successful, she hoped to be able to put on a demonstration to celebrate! She would treasure a picture of Cort smiling with pride in his family, and with gratitude to her.

One evening, Cort was absent from the dinner table. Charlie was surprised to discover how ordinary the meal seemed without his presence. She picked at her food and listened shamelessly to Marita's conversation with Jim, hoping one of them would mention Cort's whereabouts. She missed seeing him even though he rarely spoke to her. After their confrontation in his study, he had seemed to mellow somewhat. Often, she found his eyes on her, but he always turned away when her gaze made contact with his. The night before, however, she had watched him pace the veranda like a restless caged tiger. He was not a happy man.

When the cook served the dessert, Charlie decided to take the plunge. "Mmm, too bad Cort isn't here tonight. This flan is delicious. I've noticed what a sweet tooth he has for Delfina's desserts."

"Knowing Delfina, I'm sure she'll save some for him in the kitchen for later tonight. He is an inveterate icebox-raider when no one is looking," said Marita.

Period. Not one word about Cort's location.

Charlie took one more bite of the flan, rolling it around in her mouth to take up time before swallowing. She put down her spoon and took a sip of strong black coffee. It was too bitter for her taste. She preferred weak coffee like that brewed in the United States.

"If he works too late, I might beat him to it. You'd better instruct Delfina to hide it for safekeeping." Charlie winced. Was she actually *that* eager to know where he was?

"If you enjoy the flan, go ahead and eat as much as you like, Charlie. Cort is having dinner with an old friend at Lagazpe restaurant in the hotel tonight. I'm quite positive she'll want to spend the rest of the evening in the discotheque."

"Oh, no, don't tell me *she's* here again!" Alejandro groaned and made a face at Charlie.

"That's enough, Alejandro. You are not to make disparaging comments about your uncle's friends." Marita's voice was stern.

"Forgive me, Mama, but she is such a witch. When *Tio* Cortez isn't looking, she is forever telling me to get lost."

"That's enough, Alejandro. Why don't you excuse yourself from the table, and find something constructive to do until bedtime?"

"*Si*, Mama. There is a baseball game on television tonight, the Yankees against the Red Sox. May I watch it?"

"All right." Marita shook her head. "Boys will be boys, isn't that the old saying?"

"It was in my day," Jim agreed amiably. "I believe I'll watch a few minutes of that game with Alejandro, if you ladies will excuse me. I need to mull over a few ideas before trying to put them on paper tonight. We begin field work on the course tomorrow." Jim pushed back his chair and smiled apologetically. "I hate to break up the meal and leave you to yourselves so early, but, I'll make it up tomorrow night. Why don't I treat you to an evening out? Cort has told me what a magnificent restaurant Legazpe is. We'll celebrate ground-breaking in style, with the fanciest dinner on the menu. How does that sound?''

"Wonderful! We accept, no questions asked. Now, off with you before you change your mind." Marita sparkled, her smile so dazzling Jim seemed to be having difficulty taking his eyes off her face.

"Come on, Alejandro. We don't want to miss the first inning." He placed his arm around the boy's thin shoulders and walked with him out of the dining room, chatting companionably about baseball statistics.

Marita and Charlie watched them leave, and when they faced each other across the table again, both noticed the excess moisture accumulated in the other's eyes. "He's a very special man, isn't he?" Marita dabbed at her eyes with a corner of her napkin.

"I've always thought so," agreed Charlie softly. She picked up her spoon and finished her dessert without looking up again.

Clearing her throat, Marita attempted to resume their conversation. "I feel I should correct the poor impression of Mercedes Delgado you must have after Alejandro's comments. A child can't be expected to appreciate someone of her nature. I'm afraid he has no use for anyone unwilling to give him equal billing."

On the other hand, kids tend to be honest, Charlie told herself.

"Mercedes is a well-known Mexican film star," continued Marita. "Lately, she has become quite popular in foreign pictures. I have only seen a couple of her movies. They tend to be in the R-rated category, if you know what I mean. Personally, I don't enjoy those explicit films. I guess I'm rather old-fashioned. I prefer romance, and the use of my imagination. So many pictures made today seem to degrade the relationships between men and women which God has ordained sacred.''

"I don't get to many movies when I'm on tour, but the few I've seen recently turned me off." Charlie laughed briefly, and leaned forward to confide. "I've walked out of the last two P-G rated pictures because the language offended me. How's that for purity!"

Marita's dark eyes skimmed her face with warm approval. "You're a woman after my own heart. Jim told me you were a believer in Christ's teachings. I'm so glad. I wish you were going to stay longer. We need your good influence. Actually, I've already seen a change in Cortez. I hear him singing in his room when he arises in the mornings. It has been years since . . . well, I shouldn't discuss his private life. I've just been so concerned about him. He seemed to turn his back on God after Helena's death, but something has happened to wake him up. Perhaps it's working with Jim every day. Cort loves your father like a brother. I'm praying that Jim's wonderful faith will help him . . . but enough of that." Marita finished her coffee and stared into the empty cup in thoughtful contemplation. "We were talking about Mercedes Delgado. I have a sneaking suspicion that you won't care for her. She's one of those women whom you either admire for her beauty and talent, or dislike—"

"—for her talent and beauty! I get the picture. She probably has a figure like an hourglass and dresses it to make the most of every curve. I know the type." Charlie gestured in the air and joined Marita in appreciation of the humorous portrayal. "We're being catty. How did Cort meet the lady?"

"I'm not sure, but I think she vacationed at Las Hadas shortly after Cort purchased it. It isn't easy for a person of Mercedes' reputation to find a secluded place to rest. Most of the guests at Las Hadas are people of wealth and position, so they aren't easily impressed. Fortunately, Mercedes likes it here and returns whenever she's between films. She has contracted to buy the entire top floor of the new condominium Cort is building. Today she has come to discuss the interior decoration."

"How long will she be staying?" Charlie felt a discomforting knot in her stomach. Not many days were left before she must leave Las Hadas, and although she was enjoying herself, she had not had an opportunity to be alone with Cort. Viewed from a distance, he seemed less threatening. Perhaps they could yet have a civil conversation . . . declare a truce . . . maybe even become friends.

"Hopefully not long. I don't want her to monopolize Cort while you're here. I think it's important for us all to get to know each other well." Marita lowered her lashes under Charlie's questioning look. "I don't want you to worry about Jim while he's staying with us."

Hours later Charlie was still awake, mulling over Marita's description of Mercedes Delgado. They had both carefully avoided mentioning that Cortez could be a lonesome man, actively seeking a replacement for his wife . . . unless he felt as duty-bound to care for Marita and Alejandro as her father had been for her these past many years.

Marita was right. Charlie didn't have to meet the woman to know she would dislike her intensely.

Dear Lord, take all this anger and hatred from me! You have instructed me to love others as much as I love myself, and used Yourself as the perfect example of how far I should go in that loving. You loved even your enemies! Somehow, even when my spirit is willing, my will is weak. I have absolutely no reason to dislike this Mercedes Delgado, Lord. I don't know her. I've never seen her. But since you know so much about me already, you know how very jealous I feel that she can spend an entire evening with Cort, when he doesn't even want to spend a minute alone with me! Forgive me for getting sidetracked from seeking Your will in my life, and for talking about my host so much, but, Lord, Cortez Ruillon is on my mind incessantly!

Snapping off the lamp beside the bed, Charlie punched her pillow with unnecessary vigor and stretched out on the cool satin sheets. Thirty minutes of tossing and turning failed to dispel the vision of a voluptuous Latin siren sharing an intimate dinner for two. Disgusted, she flipped on the light.

It was bad enough that her waking hours were filled with thoughts of Cort, but she had allowed her silly infatuation to go too far. She would not spend the night dreaming about him. She needed a catharsis to purge him from her brain.

Padding across the bedroom floor in her oversized pink Izod sleep shirt, she got down on her knees to hunt for her old deerskin moccasins. Only one showed up, and Charlie tossed it into a corner impatiently.

Standing in the middle of the bedroom, she debated for another minute on the wisdom of her plan, and then cast aside her caution as easily as she had the slipper. Eating another serving of heavenly flan was the ideal method of exorcising evil spirits from her mind. At least, it was better than lying in bed.

The entire household must be asleep, and Cort was otherwise occupied for the night. She could haunt the kitchen without disturbing a single soul, and no one would be the wiser, except Delfina, who would find an empty flan dish on the counter in the morning.

Charlie crept down the hall, thankful, as her bare feet touched the first stone stair, that there could be no creaking to give her away. There was enough moonlight coming through the windows to enable her to walk without fear of bumping into things, and she reached the kitchen quickly.

The night light Delfina had left on near the sink provided just enough illumination to keep the secretive rendezvous with the flan more enjoyable. Tiptoeing with exaggerated steps across the white tile floor, Charlie pretended she was sneaking up on her unsuspecting prey. With deliberately slow motions, she placed her hand on the refrigerator handle, and inch by inch pulled open the door. When the inside light spilled out into the room, she hid behind the door and peeked cautiously around the edge. Suddenly she leaped from around the door to stand with her hands on her hips.

"Aha, you wretched flan!" she whispered. "You didn't think I'd come back, did you? Where are you hiding? Nothing can save you now." She followed the shelves with her eyes until she located the cellophane-wrapped dish beside a fresh mango. "There you are, you luscious, beautiful thing," she sighed, bending over to remove it carefully from the refrigerator. "I could never tire of you. Not in a million, trillion years."

"Nor could I."

Not until the message finally got through to her brain that her bare feet and legs were freezing, did Charlie realize she was still crouched over the flan in front of an open refrigerator. How long she had stayed transfixed, she didn't know. She straightened her back and closed the door, welcoming the swift return to semi-darkness.

Still holding the dish of flan in front of her, she closed her eyes and tried to reason with herself. The eating of flan was meant to exorcise the presence of Cort from her mind, not to conjure up a more realistic picture of him! Since when did daydreams talk back?

The hair on her arms was standing on end, and somehow she knew it had nothing to do with the oversized goose-bumps sharing the same space. With trepidation and a stiff resolve, Charlie turned toward the kitchen door.

"Cort."

Her mouth formed Cort's name, but no sound came from between her lips. A rapid, hard thumping began somewhere under the alligator emblem on the left side of her shirt. For the first time in her life, she wished she wore long-legged flannel pajamas. She wished the floor would open up and swallow her whole.

Incapable of speech or movement, she stared at Cort as he leaned against the door jamb, his tuxedo jacket over one shoulder, his tie stuffed in one pocket, his shirt open at the collar. She remembered her silly monologue and Cort's intentional distortion of its meaning. Her eyes smarted. She clenched her jaw. How he must relish her humiliation!

His amusement, at first so evident to her, changed within seconds, and her heart skipped several beats. He covered the distance between them in long strides. Taking the dish from her hands, his deep umber eyes never moved from her face. "If you drop it, we'll have to do without Delfina's treat to dream on."

A hot flush suffused her body, from the tip of her toes to the top of her scalp, and her lashes dropped to hide her eyes.

As if reading her mind and understanding her embarrassment, he continued speaking, his voice bland and conversational. "I spoke with Marita on the telephone a while ago, and she told me about the flan. I've looked forward to this moment ever since. I assume you've already discovered its merits, or you wouldn't be down here trying to rob me of one of my favorite pasttimes."

Charlie watched him place the dish on a small round table occupying a special nook at the far side of the room. He crossed to a cupboard and removed two bowls. "If you'd care to be seated, *señorita*, I'll serve." He pulled open a drawer and chose two teaspoons and a dessert spoon. "If I'm in charge, I can give myself a larger portion. Since you've already had flan tonight, it's only fair."

He turned his back to her, and walked toward another cupboard, allowing Charlie time to skitter across the tile floor and slide onto the chair across the table. She tucked her sleep shirt tightly under her thighs, crossing her legs in front of her.

Cort returned to the table with two cups of hot water, heated in the microwave oven, and a jar of instant coffee. "I like coffee with my flan," he said, juggling the cups and container while he pulled out his chair with a foot. "It's caffeine-free. Won't keep us awake."

With disarming ease, he turned an intolerable situation for Charlie into an hour of light-hearted companionship. He told her about his other resorts in Mexico, Florida, and the Bahamas, and why he had chosen Las Hadas as a place to build a house.

"Of course, I still have a home in California. I'm not a Mexican national, you know. My father was, and I inherited a *hacienda* and considerable land from him. My mother was a Texan and refused to give up her U.S. citizenship to live here permanently. That meant they had to spend several months a year in the States to keep her happy. Marita and I were born and educated there and chose to become U.S. citizens on our eighteenth birthdays. I joined the PGA soon after graduating from college. Like you, I'd been playing in golf tournaments since middle childhood, and somehow couldn't give it up in favor of business or ranching." He toyed with his spoon, and was soon lost in personal memories, apparently too painful to communicate.

"Do you miss it now?" Charlie sipped her coffee and peered at him over the rim of the cup. Sitting this closely to him, she could see the fine lines radiating from the corners of his eyes, arching upward across his temple and downward over the sun-bronzed angles of his cheeks. She resisted the urge to smooth them with the tips of her fingers.

"Not now," Cort replied, "but I did for two or three years. I've been able to compensate through my business endeavors—redesigning golf courses, or by building new ones. If the quality is there, the club attracts many of my old friends, and we get together for a few rounds . . . strictly for pleasure, of course, but I haven't lost my touch. Maybe someday we could have a round together and I can prove it." He slanted her a teasing look and winked. Her toes curled of their own volition.

"You . . . you also have a wonderful voice, Cort," she said breathlessly, immediately feeling like a star-struck teenager, and as foolish. "Have you ever sung professionally?"

"No, only in school productions, and in church . . . and for the family, of course." Cort lapsed into quiet contemplation of his spoon. "But I haven't sung anywhere for several years now."

"What a terrible shame. God has given you a rare and beautiful gift. It isn't right for you to bury it, Cort. Most of us would give our life's savings for the talent you exhibited the other evening. I was very . . . moved."

Cort's dark eyes searched her face for signs of sarcasm or mockery, and when he found none, softly murmured, "Thank you. I'll have to think about it. I haven't wanted to sing since . . ."

"It's never very easy to make decisions, is it? Our lives can be so complex, and our choices so baffling. All we can do is keep asking the Lord what He wants us to do, and take the time to listen. I've been having problems with that lately."

Charlie finished her coffee and put down her cup. The action seemed to be a signal to Cort. He placed his cup on top of the bowl, and put them into the empty flan dish. "It's getting late, and morning comes early. Guess we'd better clear these away."

Simultaneously Charlie and Cort pushed back their chairs and reached for the dirty dishes.

"I'll put these . . ." Charlie began, attempting to pick up the pile.

"You go on, and I'll . . ." Cort said, his hands closing over hers accidentally.

The space between them narrowed considerably, and every ion in the air was so highly charged that Charlie could almost hear their crackling. She kept her eyes on the dishes and prayed Cort couldn't feel her trembling.

"I was going to . . ." she resumed, glancing up with a shy smile. Her voice was unnaturally soft and breathy.

"It isn't . . ." Cort protested huskily, his gaze meeting hers.

They burst into a brief, spontaneous spurt of laughter, but as quickly as it was launched, it died. Cort's luminous black eyes scrutinized her face with disturbing thoroughness. They were alone, shrouded by only a thin veil of light, and the potency of their attraction to each other flared between them.

With unnerving deliberation, Cort brushed a wayward strand of pale silk from Charlie's face, following the motion with his eyes. "Beautiful," he mused. He touched an eyebrow, tracing its shape. Then his hand cupped her chin. "You have such lovely skin."

"I-I have freckles," she stuttered, wondering if her suddenly spineless skeleton could continue to hold her upright.

"I know. They're adorable." His eyes sought them out, and then his lips. It was only a matter of time before those same lips found hers. His kiss was soft, a brushing of butterfly wings, only a whisper of what her lips remembered. Suddenly Cort ended the caress. "Forgive me," he said, his deep voice pensive, his hand falling to her shoulder to issue an impersonal squeeze. "I didn't mean to take advantage of you." He watched her reaction, his face mere inches from hers.

"That's . . . all right," she said, her voice unsteady. "I'm not a child, remember?" She took her hands off the dishes and hugged her body. She could feel her heart throbbing.

"I remember . . . but I don't think you know much about being a woman yet."

Charlie's breathing quickened. "I . . . I don't know what you mean."

"No, I'm sure you don't." Cort chuckled deeply. "I'm not the one who should teach you, unfortunately. Good night, Charlie." He dropped a chaste kiss onto her forehead.

Before he could step away, Charlie impulsively put out a hand and touched the front of his tuxedo shirt, letting it slide upward until it met the mat of dark curly hair at the base of his throat. "Charlie, Charlie," Cort sighed, catching her hand under his and pressing it hard against his skin. "You're so young and so innocent."

She tried to speak, but was confused by his comment. She could only feel, and her feelings had no name. Both her hands crept up around his neck. Hungry for closeness, she balanced on her toes like a ballet dancer *en pointe*. A pulse hammered in her throat. For endless minutes they remained locked together, their lips only inches apart, like marble statues sculpted for eternity.

Cort was still, waiting. For the first time in her life, Charlie suspected what it must be costing him, for she, too, was tormented by the warring factions of reason and emotion. While she ached to be drawn closer, her mind screamed that such passion was not reverent love. Could she sacrifice self-respect and all the values she held dear for a moment of careless disregard?

Bracing herself for Cort's reaction, and feeling empty inside, Charlie unwrapped her arms from his neck and took a step away.

"I'm sorry," she whispered, her voice cracking. "I
. . . I think I should go up to my room now."

Cort let her go and immediately put even greater
distance between them. He cleared his throat and she
could hear the harsh rhythm of his breathing. "Good
girl," he said, turning to pick up the dishes on the
table.

"Forgive me . . ."

"Good night, Charlie."

Her bare feet made no noise on the tile floor. The
tears on her cheeks rolled mutely. A bitter laugh
stopped behind lips curled in agony. *Dear God, this is
the hardest test I've ever had to face since my mother
and brother's death. All week I've prayed for patience, and for the ability to understand what's
happening in my life. I'm hurting inside, Lord, and I
feel miserable, so teach me how to give thanks for
every experience which helps me mature in my faith
. . . even this bewildering relationship with Cort.
Where do I go from here, Lord? Please show me the
way, and light the path with such a blazing beacon
that I can't possibly miss it!*

CHAPTER 7

AFTER A NIGHT OF RESTLESSNESS and little sleep, Charlie welcomed the first signs of dawn. A creature of habit, she was accustomed to hard work. She had drifted long enough. Since she couldn't leave Manzanillo for another week, the solution was obvious. Physical activity. No more lolling on the beach, watching the tide roll in.

Dressing hastily in a stretch gabardine culotte of brilliant red, with a tattersall racing stripe across one corner, Charlie searched in a dresser drawer for the coordinating cotton shirt. Today she would dress like a pro, practice like a pro, and think like a pro. In one week she would return to the world of professional golf. She belonged there. She had worked too long and hard reaching her level of expertise, to give it up for an unappreciative male . . . be it Dean Connally or . . . or Cortez Ruillon.

During the night Charlie's common sense had returned. She had been wrong to listen to Dean. She *was* capable of loving a man other than her father, and she had infinite passion to give. She knew that now.

She was neither cold, as Dean had implied, nor a spoiled, clinging child, as Cort had intimated.

She was a woman, with all of the normal yearnings and needs of any woman. But she was a Christian, too, and was only now realizing how that prior commitment affected all other relationships in life. It wasn't an easy lesson.

Meanwhile, God's special gift to her—the star quality of her athletic ability—might prove to be the answer to her predicament with Cort. She would simply go on developing the gift and enjoying the success it created, remembering to give God the credit. She had a right to seek continued achievement, and to wait for a man who could love her unconditionally. This had to be God's will for her life, or He would never have allowed her to achieve so much, so quickly.

Pulling the visor of her red baseball cap over her quickly combed curls, she inched the bedroom door open and sneaked out with the stealth of a cat.

By the time Charlie reached the clubhouse, she was completely energized. During the brisk walk, she had concluded that all the best years lay ahead of her, and that good things come to those with the patience to wait . . . maybe even a man—the right man. After all, twenty-six was not old. She had plenty of time.

It had always bothered her to hear friends on the tour complaining about dating. Most of them were single and, while they might be attracted to the good-looking guys in the galleries, they realized short-term friendships were usually a waste of time. Within three days, they would move on to another location.

Relationships were difficult enough to establish, and great distances tended to attenuate them quickly. The girls—women—who complained the most were generally those who had lost sight of their ultimate goal—to be a consistent winner, to be the best woman golfer in the world.

Charlie entered the clubhouse with a cheery greeting for Diego Ortiz, the manager. She had been aware of his silent appraisal, and had often caught his eyes on her while teaching on the driving range; but, because Marita and Alejandro had usually been with her, she had not had an opportunity to chat with him about their mutual interest in golf.

"Good morning, Señor Ortiz. Is it too early for me to use the greens?"

"*Buenas dias* , Señorita Summers." Diego's soft brown eyes registered surprise at her early appearance, but his grin of welcome compensated nicely. He pushed back an unruly shock of black hair.

"Call me Charlie, please. Everyone does."

"Call me Diego, then. Everyone does."

They laughed, falling into an easy banter while Diego opened her locker and withdrew the bag of clubs on loan for her use. He watched as she laced up her golf shoes.

"I've been wondering how many days it would take for you to get serious about your game again. Pretending it doesn't matter when it does is tough to do, isn't it?"

"You said it," Charlie agreed. "Where do we get some of our crazy ideas? I suppose you heard about my brilliant plan to quit the tour a couple weeks ago."

Diego sat beside her on the bench fronting the row of lockers, and leaned on his knees. "I read about it in *Golf Digest*. Quitting never works, you know. I knew you'd go back."

"It worked for Cortez," she countered.

"It was different for him. Everyone thought he had a chance to be one of the best, but playing on the tour was only a game for him. It came too easily. There was no burning challenge, no hunger to reach the top."

Charlie gave him a quick appraisal. "Is he hungry now?"

109

"You're mocking me, Charlie, but I speak the truth. Cort found his proper niche when he decided to develop vacation properties into first-class golfing resorts. Las Hadas is a masterpiece, the summit of his unquestionable success. He's ready for something else now, I think."

"Are you an amateur psychologist on the side, Diego?"

"It doesn't take a special degree to see the man isn't happy. He needs a wife and family. His sister and nephew are family, of course, but it isn't the same. He has all of the responsibilities, but none of the pleasures." He gave her a lazy sidelong glance. "That's an old saying, you know."

Charlie grinned. "I know, Diego," she said, making a face. "I didn't just fall off a turnip truck!"

Diego gave her a quizzical look. "Now you have succeeded in bewildering me. What is this turnip truck?"

"It means I am not an uneducated peasant. I know what you meant. Let's change the subject. I think Señor Ruillon's personal life is his own business, not ours." Charlie hoisted her bag of golf clubs onto her shoulder. She felt a need to avoid any further discussion of Cortez. In spite of her decision to ignore him from now on, remembrances of the previous evening were still too fresh in her mind. "I'm off to perfect my game, or I won't have a choice to make. If I lose my touch, I might be permanently retired."

"Would you like some company?"

Charlie turned at the door. "Don't you have to mind the store?"

"In five minutes, Juan will be here to take charge. My morning is free."

"I'm not sure I can afford your instruction. What is a golf pro's fee in Mexico?"

"If the pupil is pretty enough, he usually settles

110

for a lemonade by the pool. If she gives him too much grief, he might demand her company during lunch."

"I can afford that. You're on."

"Good. Go ahead and warm up on the driving range. I'll meet you there as soon as I give Juan his instructions."

The morning passed quickly. Diego proved an invaluable help, and offered Charlie several good tips on the use of her sand wedge, a difficult club for her if she allowed it to intimidate her.

Not once during the two rounds of nine holes, did Charlie think of Cortez, or their encounter in the kitchen of the villa. It all came tumbling back, however, when Alejandro met her in the clubhouse, demanding explanations.

"Where have you been, Charlie? I looked everywhere for you. Uncle Cort said you didn't show up for breakfast because you were probably tired after last night, but Mama checked in your room, and you weren't there. We were worried. Aren't we going to play golf now? Why did you go off without me?"

Diego grinned and pulled the brim of his hat down over his eyes with a gentle tug. "Hold on there, Alejandro. You're talking a mile a minute. Does Señorita Summers need to check in with you before she begins her day?"

"That's all right, Diego. I've been instructing Alejandro and his mother and completely forgot to leave them a note this morning. Forgive me, Alejandro. I needed to put in some extra work practicing this morning, and the time slipped away from me. We'll go have a lesson right now. Is Marita coming, too?" She slid a look of apology to Diego. "May I take a rain check on that lemonade?"

"Tonight, when I close the Club?"

"What time is that?"

"About six o'clock. We could make it a mai tai instead."

"I don't drink alcohol, Diego, but I never seem to get enough of the wonderful fruit concoctions here. Where shall I meet you?"

"How about the lagoon terrace?"

"I'll look forward to it." Charlie draped her arm over Alejandro's shoulder. "Come on, pal. Let's go practice with your putter today."

As they strolled down the sidewalk to the putting green, Alejandro peered up at Charlie, a look of concern causing a deep furrow between his eyes. "Is Señor Ortiz your sweetheart, Charlie?"

"Of course not. He's a very fine golf instructor. He gave me some lessons this morning, that's all."

"I thought you were already a professional, Charlie. You don't need any more lessons."

"Even professionals need an occasional refresher, Alejandro, and they always need lots and lots of practice. If I'm going to go back on the tour, I can't let myself get rusty."

Alejandro thought for a few seconds before he answered. "I think Señor Ortiz would like to have you for a sweetheart, Charlie. He watches you all the time. I see him stare at you when we are here every morning."

"You're imagining things, Alejandro. He's watching to make sure I don't teach you the wrong things. When I leave Las Hadas, he'll continue with your lessons."

"I don't want you to leave, Charlie. Can't you stay here with your father?" Alejandro slipped his hand into Charlie's.

"You're sweet to suggest it, but I don't think your uncle needs another mouth to feed on a permanent basis, do you?"

"You could marry Uncle Cortez. Mama tells him all the time he should have a wife. You like it here, don't you, Charlie?"

In her mind's eyes, Charlie envisioned herself as

Cort's wife. He would be very demanding, shamelessly possessive, and gloriously passionate. "Of course I do. I love it here. It's the most beautiful place I've ever seen, but I can't stay here. I have to work to support myself. Your uncle must find himself a wife without your help, Alejandro. A man likes to choose for himself. You'll do the same some day."

"Not me. I'm going to live with my mama forever, and take care of her."

"That's nice, Alejandro. Your mama is a lucky lady."

"I know. That's what she says. I'm going to ask *Tio* Cortez if he'll take care of you. Then you won't have to go away to work." They had reached the practice green, and Alejandro busied himself by pouring out the golf balls from the bucket provided by the club.

"Please, don't do that, Alejandro." Charlie was in a panic. Why did kids have to have such big ears, such busy mouths, and such zany ideas!

"But yesterday you told me to do it."

"I don't mean the golf balls, pal. I mean, please don't say anything to Cort about taking care of me."

"Why?"

"Never mind. Just don't." Charlie smiled enticingly. "Let's concentrate on getting the balls into the holes now. Remember what I taught you?"

"Yes. I should bend down and look at the grass between the hole and the ball. I should see if there are any little hills, or slopes, or valleys that would make the ball turn. I should try to stroke the ball into a small circle around the hole. Then, I will be sure to get it in on my second try." He hunched his shoulders, pleased with his recitation, and waited for her approval.

"If I had a gold star, I would paste it right here, pal. You're a good listener." Charlie laughed and kissed him on the nose. "Now, let's see how well you can do."

They practiced for an hour, and on the walk back to the villa, Charlie dabbed at her misting eyes with her knuckle. She would miss Alejandro. He was as lovable, and as loving, as any young child could possibly be. He would make a wonderful little brother.

Although she had hurried, taking a quick shower before donning a clean safari shorts set and pink espadrilles, everyone else was already seated in the dining room when she arrived. Cort rose politely to pull out her chair, and she felt herself flush with the flicking of his dark eyes across her still-damp hair.

"Sorry I'm so late," she murmured.

"You mustn't think it necessary to rush, dear." Marita took a sip of her iced tea and put it down to add another teaspoon of sugar. "Alejandro kept us entertained with an accounting of your activity this morning."

Charlie darted a quick glance at a grinning set of impish brown eyes peeking behind a glass of pink lemonade. What had the little rascal told them? "I wish I had been here to defend myself. I can only hope it was accurate."

"It was," interjected her young partner. "I told them you had missed breakfast because you had a date with Señor Ortiz this morning. They were laughing and joking so much they didn't even see me until they were all the way inside the clubhouse, *Tio* Cortez. That man sure is stuck on Charlie. And he's going to see her again tonight . . . six o'clock by the pool terrace."

"Alejandro!" Marita's reminder stopped his chatter midstream, and her scowl forbade him to continue. "Diego Ortiz is a charming young man, Charlie, and from what Cort has said in the past, a teaching pro of great ability."

"I was impressed with his skill and knowledge. If I didn't already have a caddy, I'd try to steal him from you. I wonder why he hasn't tried to go professional himself." Charlie fussed with her food, moving it around on her plate.

"He came from a poor family and wasn't able to find the financial backing necessary to work his way up through the ranks. He was introduced to me by my caddy when I played on the PGA, and after I bought this resort, I hired him to be my club pro and manager." Cort spoke in a matter-of-fact tone of voice, as though he found the entire subject boring.

"Diego was a lucky find for you. I'm eager for Dad to talk with him. I think he has some interesting ideas about the new course. Where is Dad, by the way?" Charlie fought to stay as detached and emotionless as Cort. Last night was an average, run-of-the-mill occurrence for him, as meaningless an activity as kissing babies for a politician on the campaign trail.

"I suspect that, for the next few days, food is going to be the farthest thing from Jim's mind. The earth movers have arrived, and Jim is collaborating extensively with his engineer." Cort occupied himself with buttering a flour tortilla.

"Poor darling. He'll be starved before dinner tonight. We'll be kind to him, and provide substantial appetizers during tea-time." Marita patted her lips with the starched white napkin from her lap, and addressed her brother with a touch on his arm. "Are you planning to join us for dinner tonight, Cort dear? Jim has invited us to Legazpe for an evening of frivolity."

"He asked me to make up a foursome, and I accepted. We leave here at eight o'clock. Why don't we meet in the garden room at seven?"

Charlie felt Cort's eyes on her again, and heard the slight emphasis he placed on the time. "Oh, good," she said, with feigned enthusiasm. "I'll have plenty of time to spend with Diego. You can enjoy those appetizers without me here, can't you, Marita?"

"Perhaps you should postpone your social hour with Ortiz until another evening, Charlie." Cort spoke without looking up.

"There's always tomorrow, Cort. Diego promised to help me with my wedge in the morning. Don't worry about me, please. I can tell time. I'll be ready by eight sharp." Charlie spoke brightly, resenting Cort's interference in her life. His disapproval of her plans made her all the more determined to follow through with them. It bothered her that she could be so strong-willed and decisive—*until she was near him*.

Cort pushed his chair from the table. "I'll be in my office most of the afternoon, Marita."

"That's fine, dear." She smiled at him with a look of infinite tenderness. He responded by pressing a kiss to her forehead and murmuring words of endearment in Spanish. "And I thought Alejandro and I would stop in the village to visit Rosa and her daughter this afternoon. It would give Charlie some time to herself. *Tio* Cortez told me Rosa's brother, Manuel, was visiting them, Alejandro. He's the famous matador from Mexico City, remember?"

Alejandro moved quickly from the table. "A real matador, Mama? Will he give me his autograph?"

"If you ask politely, I don't think he will refuse."

"I'll get one for you, too, Charlie!" Alejandro flung the last words over his shoulder as an afterthought. He was already out the door of the dining room and on the way to his room.

Two hours later Charlie moved restlessly on the chaise lounge by the lagoon-sized swimming pool surrounded and shadowed by tall palm trees. She had given up on her attempt to read, and sleep continued to elude her, even though she was bone-tired.

Deep inside, a voice suggested an alternative reason for her edginess. Unless she kept her eyes closed, it was impossible to avoid seeing the endless spectacle of romantic couples. They surrounded her in the pool, around the pool, at the bar, on the beach, everywhere. None of them appeared to be having difficulty forgetting work and responsibilities. With each caress, each kiss, each entwined hand she witnessed, her own restlessness increased. She was sick of it.

Back in her room, Charlie paced the floor. Suddenly decisive, she crossed the room to the telephone and asked the operator to dial her agent, Donn Marcus, in Palm Springs. Thirty minutes later she replaced the receiver and danced across the room to flop across the bed. Donn had assured her she would be welcome back on the tour with no problems to overcome. He had been in constant contact with the LPGA managers and directors, who had been hopeful for just such a miracle.

With her future assured, she could concentrate on living through one more week at Las Hadas. If there were only some way to leave sooner. Leaping off the bed, she tried one more call . . . to the airport at Manzanillo.

For the next two hours, Charlie prepared herself for the evening. She wanted it to be a memorable one. She washed her hair and used a conditioner to restore the sheen and softness robbed by the exposure to the sea and sun.

She chose one of her favorite evening outfits—a red, silk-jersey jumpsuit, slit to reveal her long legs as she moved. It was sensuous, surprising, and shape-revealing. It was preposterously daring. It was perfect for the occasion. Perfect for making one last, lingering impression of a *woman* . . . not a female athlete.

Smiling at her image in the mirror, Charlie dabbed White Shoulders perfume behind her earlobes and on her wrists. Stepping back, she took one final look, shaking her softly curled hair about her own white shoulders. Making a sudden decision, she removed the pearl studs from her ears and exchanged them for elaborate, dangle earrings of eighteen-karat gold and diamonds—a gift from her agent for her twenty-first birthday.

Tucking a comb and lipstick into her copper metallic evening bag, a new purchase made to accompany her matching slings, she turned out the lamp on the dresser, and moved toward the entrance of her room. As her hand touched the knob, someone tapped lightly on the door.

Carlos, the houseman, stood in the hall outside with a look of open admiration on his face. "Yes? May I help you?" Pleased with the first reaction to her appearance, Charlie was generous with her smile.

"*Si*, Señorita Summers." Carlos's lustrous brown eyes danced. "You have received a message from Señor Ortiz. There has been an emergency. He will be unable to meet you."

Charlie sobered immediately, and frowned. "I don't understand, Carlos. Did Señor Ortiz call on the telephone? Why didn't he ask to speak with me?"

"I cannot say, *señorita* . He asked his assistant to place the call on our special intercom system. It is quicker that way."

"You're certain he said he couldn't meet me at all?"

"*Si, señ orita*. You wish to send a message in return?"

"No. That won't be necessary, Carlos. Thank you for taking the trouble to come up here."

"No trouble, *señorita*. It was a pleasure!"

Charlie flashed him a stilted smile, ignoring his cheeky compliment. Closing the door, she tossed her purse onto the bed and walked thoughtfully to the window. She paused there, peering blindly at the languid aquamarine bay soaking up the changing pastel colors produced by the setting sun, her disappointment too acute to dismiss lightly.

She was all dolled up with no place to go for two whole hours! If she were more of an adventuress, she would go somewhere by herself. Well, why not? She was in a reckless mood. Independent ladies could do whatever they pleased, whenever they pleased. They didn't need escorts. Not in the eighties!

CHAPTER 8

ONCE AGAIN, CHARLIE TOOK UP her purse and headed for the door of her room. This time she breezed down the stairs, her high-heeled slings clicking a carefree staccato. Squelching guilt feelings over her plans to deceive both her father and the Ruillons again, she consoled herself with plausible excuses. She was not sneaking out of the house, and they knew she had previous plans.

"Are you off to meet Ortiz, Charlie?"

Charlie whirled. Cortez stood in the doorway of his study, his dark eyes appraising her with lazy insouciance. "Yes, well, actually I . . ."

A wing of Cort's eyebrow arched, and his sable eyes glinted with curiosity. Charlie's stomach lurched. She had always found fibbing impossible, and now her indecision had aroused his suspicion. "Why are you dressed so early, Cort?" she asked quickly, hoping to divert his interest in her answer.

"I have a brief business meeting at Las Hadas. Is Ortiz planning to pick you up, or are you meeting him?"

"He's . . . ah . . . he's not picking me up." That was the absolute truth, so why was she tongue-tied?

"He's meeting you at the lagoon terrace then. I'll drive you there in my car. It's too far for you to walk in those flimsy shoes." Cort moved toward her, a knockout smile lighting his mahogany face.

Charlie protested weakly, her nerves on edge, her heart now skipping beats, and her confidence rapidly eroding. "No, Cort, that isn't necessary. I planned on walking there by myself. I wouldn't dream of inconveniencing you."

"It's on my way. Come on. Carlos has driven the car out front." He took her by the elbow and propelled her out the front door of the villa.

"*No*, Cortez. I want to walk!" Charlie pulled free.

"Why must you be so stubborn?" Cort's deep voice teased her on a note of impatient amusement. "Please let me be a good host and escort you to your date. You are far too beautiful tonight to go there on your own."

The casual compliment and expression of concern for her safety were her undoing. "All right then," she conceded, reluctant to explain that her date had been cancelled. She avoided looking at Cort and preceded him out the entrance and down the wide marble stairs to the waiting car. If he touched her arm again, she would fall to pieces.

Cort reached around her and opened the door of the white convertible. He watched without comment as she slid onto the low bucket seat, smoothing the folds of the red jumpsuit under her before settling. As the garment was constructed to do, the back pleat of one leg fell open, exposing the full length of her slender leg from mid-thigh to ankle, where the fabric buttoned in a wide cuff. Cort leaned forward to place the fragile material up over her leg in order to close the car door.

"Poor Diego," he crooned, his slumberous eyes slanting her a look which sent her senses reeling.

Elated over the success of her unconventional *haute couture* costume, Charlie asked coyly, "Why, 'poor Diego'?"

"Because you aren't playing fair with him. He doesn't stand a chance tonight, and you know it." Cort's low-pitched voice caused a rapid acceleration of her pulse.

"Oh? A chance for what?" She was slowly drowning in the deep ebony pools of Cort's eyes, but she invited his critique with a sparkle of mischief in her blue-violet ones, and a subtle twitching of her moist lips.

Charlie waited with bated breath for his response. He disappointed her by abruptly leaving to walk around to the driver's side of the car, and sliding in beside her without comment.

He started the motor and pushed the shift stick into first gear, pausing to meet her inquisitive eyes. "Diego will take one look at you in this provocative outfit you have chosen to wear tonight, and fall like a ton of bricks, Charlie. Is that what you intended—to have him fall in love with you?"

Charlie's eyes fell under his intense scrutiny. She played with the diamond dinner ring on her right hand. "No, of course not." Part of her rejoiced in Cort's admission that he found her attractive; the other was angry with his interference. "But, actually, it's none of your business what I choose to do . . . or Diego's, either."

Cortez was strangely quiet for several seconds, and Charlie sneaked a look at him from the corner of her eye. He was staring straight ahead through the windshield. "I'm afraid it is," he said finally, his voice cool and strong. "You are my guest, and Diego is my employee. I can't stand by and see you make fools of each other on a whim."

"You're making judgments again. I won't have it, Cort!"

"You have no choice, my impetuous young beauty," he replied starting the cart in a slow, smooth roll down the lengthy driveway. He threw her a quick look of apology. "I should have put the top up to protect your hairdo, but I'll drive carefully. Sit back and relax, because I intend to share a soda with you and Diego as your chaperone. With me along, he won't think you got all spruced up for his benefit alone."

"Take me back to the villa, Cortez. I've changed my mind."

"And leave Ortiz stranded? I couldn't be a party to that."

"He won't be there."

"How do you know?"

"He called and cancelled. He had an emergency of some kind."

"Oh? Then why did you tell me you were meeting him?"

"I didn't. I said he wasn't picking me up."

"You were going to the lagoon by yourself."

"Yes, I was. It's a family facility, and safe as a church. I was dressed and didn't want to sit around for two hours doing nothing."

"I see."

When Cort showed no sign of heading for home, Charlie rotated to stare at him, a deep scowl marring her lovely face, her pique at having no voice in the matter rising by the second.

"It took you long enough to tell me," Cort said. He grinned rather slyly, in Charlie's opinion, and something about his look told her he had set her up.

"You *knew!*" she flared, at once rebellious and ready to do battle all over again. "You let me go on, and all the time you already knew Diego wouldn't be there! I wouldn't put it past you to have engineered the whole thing!"

When Cort didn't answer, Charlie continued. "You

did, didn't you? Why?'' She watched as he maneu-
vered the elegant car through the vine-covered arch-
way and into the compound of Las Hadas Hotel,
parking under the marquee marking the entrance to
the lobby.

He stopped the motor and leaned one arm against
the steering wheel. ''Let's just say I did what I
thought was best, for the sake of an old friend.''

A young bellhop, dressed from head to toe in white,
opened the car door for Charlie, and she hesitated,
not completely understanding Cort's explanation, and
undecided about whether she should insist on his
taking her back to the villa.

''If you can find it in your heart to forgive me,
Charlie, I would very much enjoy your company for
the next hour. Marita and Jim are meeting us here at
eight for dinner.''

''Do I have a choice?''

''Of course. If you'd prefer waiting elsewhere, I'll
take you.''

Charlie made a point of reading the time on the
delicate gold watch decorating her wrist. ''We're here
now. I might as well stay,'' she said begrudgingly. ''In
the future, I would appreciate being consulted in
advance.'' She slid off the car seat, careful to keep the
pantsuit legs from parting. Already she was feeling a
little foolish for wearing the outfit. Perhaps it didn't
really fit her new lifestyle at all.

Cort offered his arm and, reluctantly, she took it.
Walking through the lobby she became conscious of
the glances cast in their direction. Cort called greetings to several people as he led her toward his office,
and she suddenly found herself jealously assessing her
competition, and feeling much too proud over being
his date for the evening.

The warm strength of Cort's hand settled over hers
as he leaned toward her in an intimate closeness.
''Would you mind waiting here for a few minutes
while I have that brief meeting? I won't be long.''

Charlie's heart drummed against her ribs, triggering a wave of giddiness. It was infantile to respond with such abandon to a person's appearance. She was far too old for a school girl crush! "No . . . I-I'll wait."

Cort had to press even closer to hear her breathless reply, and when he squeezed her hand, it took all her control to keep from tripping. Her legs felt as if they had turned to rubber, leaving them weak and almost inoperable.

During Cort's absence, Charlie talked long and hard to herself. She reviewed her purpose in dressing so outrageously, and the effects of the surprise announcement she planned to make later in the evening. It would all come to naught if she couldn't control her reactions to Cort's presence. From that moment on she must maintain a dignified coolness, a carefree nonchalance, and an utterly *temper-free* maturity.

Two hours later, as she followed Marita and Jim to their table in the luxurious restaurant, Lagazpe, she congratulated herself on her success. It hadn't been easy, but she had accomplished her goals by avoiding a direct glance at her ultra-virile, far too handsome escort. Sipping her fruit punch slowly, she had chatted casually on several safe subjects, and kept her eyes in constant motion around the dimly lit interior of the lounge.

As soon as the four of them were seated at a remote table, close enough to see and hear the orchestra, but far enough away to converse with ease, Marita touched Charlie's arm to catch her attention. "Did you notice that absolutely everyone in the room watched your entrance, Charlie? It's a shame you can't wear that gorgeous outfit on the golf course. You'd win by default every time. No one could concentrate, and your competition would be green with envy."

Charlie laughed happily with Marita. "I must confess I sometimes wear this particular outfit when I need a morale-builder following a miserable tournament loss."

"I wish I could wear something like that, but I'm too short. One should have long legs to make the most of that costume."

The waiter brought the menus, and while they read the extensive listing, the mellow strains of violin music blended magically with dim candle light and the attar of fresh roses to create an aura of enchantment far removed from reality. Charlie fought the ambiance by reading every detail on the menu with forced deliberation.

— "Cortez, *darling!* "

When the unfamiliar voice floated toward the foursome, Charlie's eyes froze on Prime Rib, *au jus*. A gentle nudge on her knee from Marita increased her sense of impending disaster.

Cort and Jim rose simultaneously to greet the most beautiful creature Charlie had ever seen in person. The woman was the antithesis of Marilyn Monroe in coloring only. Otherwise, every exquisite feature on her professionally made-up face, every luscious, seductive curve of her well-proportioned body was the same.

"Close your mouth, Charlie," Marita whispered.

Mercedes Delgado undulated around several tables, but she hardly needed the exaggerated movements to clear the chairs occupied by the entranced diners. She had gained their attention with her first greeting called across the room. Now she approached Cort with outstretched arms, speaking in rapid Spanish.

"I am so happy to see you here tonight, my darling! Providence is with me." She walked into his arms, pressing against him with familiarity, and raising her inviting lips for his kiss. "Mmm," she cooed, running her slender fuschia-tipped nails over his shoulders. "I forget from day to day how perfect a physical specimen you are, and how devastating you look in a dinner jacket."

Mercedes turned, with dark eyes fully ablaze, to give her attention to Jim. "Have we met, darling?"

"Jim Summers, may I present one of Mexico's talented stars, Mercedes Delgado." Cort introduced them in English, his mouth turned up ever so slightly in scarcely concealed humor.

"Charmed, I'm sure, Señor Summers." Mercedes offered Jim her limp hand, and Charlie sucked in her cheeks to keep from laughing aloud as she watched him bend to bestow the expected kiss of adoration. Jim didn't enjoy being in the limelight, and his face reddened. "Are you and your young wife guests at Las Hadas?" Mercedes twinkled, her English accent disgustingly attractive.

"Jim and his *daughter*, Charline, are personal friends, and house guests, Mercedes. Jim is the designer of my new golf course, and Charlie is a professional golfer in the United States."

"Charlie?" she questioned, with the merest hint of disdain. Her thick, mascara-darkened lashes brushed against the mauve shadow painted above her lids as her eyes widened to emulate utter bewilderment.

"My daughter is known as Charlie to her friends," explained Jim, shifting from one foot to another, and placing one hand into his jacket pocket for something to do.

"I see. It is rather . . . unconventional . . . the name, so . . . *macho,* I believe we could say, ¿*como?* I know next to nothing about these women's athletics." She grimaced prettily at each of the men, barely putting the hint of a wrinkle across her finely modeled nose. She finished her much practiced performance by smoothing one hand over her skin-tight, black Galanos gown. The hand, and the gown, faithfully followed her curvaceous contour, as did the eyes of every diner within easy view.

Without missing a beat, Mercedes turned to Marita, a blazing white smile never changing while she spoke.

"Señora Granado, it is lovely to see you again. How is your adorable young son?"

"He's fine, Mercedes. Charlie has been teaching him to golf while visiting with us this week. Her patience with him has worked wonders for his self-esteem, and I'm afraid he will miss her sorely when she leaves. Alejandro is determined to be a professional like Charlie some day." Marita's voice became motherly and chatty, as though she were comparing notes with her best friend or neighbor, but her references to Charlie were intentional.

"My goodness, won't that be something? Do give him a great big hug from me, won't you, dear? I love him so."

Charlie moved restlessly in her chair. The lady wasn't the least bit convincing. She loved Alejandro about as much as she loved being ignored. What she loved, was *herself*. She hated competition . . . including that from a hitherto ignored female athlete.

Mercedes' eyes lingered on Marita deliberately, and then almost as an afterthought, flitted impersonally to Charlie. She was too well-bred to be completely rude. "You must be . . . Charlie. How do you do?" She tilted her head at an arrogant angle, and her voice dripped saccharin.

Well aware she was receiving a thorough appraisal and coming up short, Charlie felt duty-bound to make a stand for female athletes everywhere. She extended a slender, sun-bronzed arm, with a dangling, unequivocally feminine hand, and compelled Mercedes to accept it in a formal handshake. She made the movie star take an aggressive role by keeping her fingers lifeless, as she had seen Mercedes do with her father.

"Charmed, I'm sure," Charlie murmured, a la Mercedes, her soft voice a perfect Vassar imitation.

Prolonging the gesture much longer than necessary, she was able to control the amount of time Mercedes had to devote to her. Satisfied she was in charge, she finally released her hand, collected her evening bag, and rose from her chair. "I do hope you will excuse me, ladies and gentlemen. I simply must go powder my nose. Cort and I were so deeply involved in our little *private* tête-a-tête before you joined us, I missed an opportunity to repair my make-up."

Charlie knew she had succeeded in insinuating an intimate relationship when Marita hid a smile behind her water glass, when her father shook his head in utter disbelief, and when Cort scowled darkly.

Charlie had only begun. Pressing herself against Cort's muscular arm, she peered up at him and intoned, "Be back in a wink, *darling*. Don't go 'way!" Then, slithering between the tables, her elegant harem pants separating with each step, she made certain every eye in the dining room could see the perfection of her bared legs . . . especially those of Señorita Delgado.

The entire act was in such brazen distaste, Charlie had difficulty keeping her composure. Her heart became a trip hammer, and her dry mouth caused her lips to stick permanently against her teeth in an insipid smile. What had once seemed like a good idea, in retrospect became a childish display.

Inside the ladies' room, Charlie headed for the first vanity chair and slumped into it with her face in her hands. For interminable seconds she listened to the sounds of her labored breathing, too ashamed to look at her face in the mirror. What in the world had possessed her to do such a zany thing? Injured pride? Why should it bother her what one prejudiced female thought of her, or of any other female athlete in the world? Who cared what the Mercedes Delgadoes of the world thought about anything?

Charline Summers did.

Why?

Because she thought Cortez Ruillon did, and it made her helplessly jealous.

Why?

Because the sight of another woman in his arms, the sight of another woman's lips on his, hurt like the slowly burning torture of sand ground deeper and deeper into an open heel blister during a tournament.

Why?

Because she didn't want Cortez Ruillon to look at, or appreciate, or talk to, or touch, or kiss, or *love* anyone but her!

Charlie drew a painful breath and faced herself in the mirror. There it was in a nutshell—the basic truth causing all the turmoil during this one week at Las Hadas. Although she had refuted its possibility in a million discussions with friends in the past, she— Charline Summers, LPGA champion—had fallen head over heels in love *at first sight* . . . with Cortez Ruillon.

She kept insisting to everyone she was old enough to know what she wanted. She believed with all her heart that love for a man was spiritual; marriage, a lifetime commitment. She had waited and longed for a man who could love her in the same way, and treat her with respect . . . never as an object to be manipulated or exploited, or to be disposed of at will.

Now she had allowed herself to fall in love with Cortez Ruillon, and she had no idea yet if he were the man God had chosen for her. She was still an immature Christian . . . willful, selfish, and temperamental. How could she expect to marry such a man and share contentment of any kind, when she always put herself and her personal feelings first He must be vastly amused by her latest show. It was about as juvenile as one could get.

Charlie drummed on the vanity with her fingers. She didn't see any way the Lord could have a hand in this latest love of hers. In all likelihood, it was another false alarm. She had once convinced herself she loved Dean, when in reality, she had singled him out as a safe security blanket. It had made her feel normal to be desired by an attractive male. Now, with Dean out of her life, and the possibility of losing her father to Marita, she had unconsciously transferred her affections to the first available male . . . a man several years her senior, *a widower*. Once she was removed from Las Hadas, she would forget all about Cort.

Balderdash!

There was more to her love for Cort than the aching physical desire she felt in simply looking at him. She fantasized herself as his wife—helping him in his work, sharing his problems, eliminating a few lines from his face, bringing joy back into his life, and perhaps even giving him children of his own.

Charlie flushed and dropped her eyes. She groped in her evening bag for her lipstick. Indulging in wishful thinking was a waste of time. She had merely succumbed to the magic spell Las Hadas cast on its unwitting guests. Tomorrow, when she returned to Palm Springs, it would be business as usual. But this time, she must work harder at giving the Lord her burdens, and trust in Him to provide the right solutions. She must commit her talent, her life, and her future to Him, and wait with greater patience for Him to reveal His plans, rather than informing Him what she wanted. Victories were rarely instantaneous.

"Charlie, dear, are you all right?" Marita dropped onto the chair next to her with a look so sympathetic and concerned that Charlie wanted to bawl out loud.

"Of course, Marita. I'm just kicking myself over that miserable performance. Thank goodness the reporters missed it!" She forced a smile. "What's going on out there?" Charlie gestured with her head, and applied another coating of color to her lips. "Is Dad terribly upset with me? He has a right to be. Is . . . is Mercedes still there?"

"Jim is bewildered, I'd say, but men rarely understand why we women do things the way we do. You don't need to hide in here, Charlie. Most of the regular dinner guests understood your behavior. I received several thumbs-up signs on my way here from those who have experienced Mercedes' antics firsthand. Cort has taken her to another restaurant. Come join your father and me in that celebration dinner. We ordered for you, and the salad has already arrived."

Relief over not having to face Cort after her self-admittance of love for him diluted Charlie's jealousy over losing him to Mercedes for the evening. She returned to the table with Marita, and made up her mind to enjoy the quiet conversation, the serenity of the dinner music atmosphere, and the excellence of the food and service. When coffee was served, she surprised Jim with the announcement, "This has really been a farewell dinner for me, as well as a celebration of your ground-breaking, Dad. I will be leaving Las Hadas tomorrow."

She was proud of the way he controlled his shock. "I'll miss you, honey. Do you have any particulars you can share with me?"

"I called Donn Marcus this afternoon and told him I missed touring. Golf is what I know best. It's the talent God has given me. I learned this week that being the best in something, working for goals, achieving them, and having the pride of accomplishment is important to God as well as to me. I'm not sure yet how He intends to use my talent for His glory, but I'll never learn it by sitting around waiting for a special vision. Right now, I feel I should devote my time and energy to becoming one of the all-time greats in women's sports. Perhaps I can be an inspiration to young girls who need encouragement in pursuing an athletic career. I'd like to be remembered forever as the Mickey Wright, the Patty Berg, the Babe Zaharias of my generation. I also want my name in the LPGA Hall of Fame as a symbol to women that when you persist, you can make it to the top. I don't think such a goal is contrary to being a Christian.''

Charlie stopped for a long, indrawn breath. "So,'' she sighed, "I'm going back on tour next week. Fortunately, I'm still wanted.''

"Of course you are,'' Jim concurred readily. "I want you to know and believe, Charlie, that I have every confidence you will succeed. If you want it, if you work for it, you'll get it. God helps those who help themselves. My only caution in the way of fatherly advice, is to keep your mind and heart open to other avenues of self-expression. Life, at its best and most rewarding, is not one-sided. Your mother had a lovely way of explaining it. She called life 'beef stew' . . . a little of this, a little of that, all blended together in a marvelous concoction that sticks to your ribs and provides nourishment for every part of your body and soul. Even the onions have an important role. Since she left us, I think we've limited ourselves mostly to meat and potatoes, honey girl, and not enough of the other good things that go with it.''

Charlie bit hard on her bottom lip, and sucked in a long breath through flared nostrils. Legazpe restaurant was no place to cry. "It's not too late for us, Dad,'' she said softly, bring his work-roughened hand to her cheek. "I won't forget, if you won't.'' Her eyes challenged him with unspoken, but pointed, meaning.

His answering look was filled with infinite pride, tenderness, understanding, encouragement and love. 'We'll compare notes in a few weeks. Okay?''

"You're on.'' Charlie kissed his palm and closed his fingers over it. "Save this for a special occasion. I love you, Dad.''

"If you two don't stop soon, I'm going to sob like a baby right here,'' said Marita in a thick voice. Her rich brown eyes were luminous with unshed tears, and her full terra-cotta lips were quivering with emotion.

"Forgive us, Marita. Why don't we pack up and

return to the villa? It doesn't seem as though Cort is going to make it back here, and suddenly, I'm not quite in the mood for dessert. Would you mind?'' Jim laid his hand over hers on the table and his eyes were as gentle as his request.

''Of course not, Jim. You need to spend some time in private with Charlie tonight.''

In the car, Marita leaned closer to Charlie. ''I hope you won't mind if I try to stir a few Mexican herbs into your father's stew.''

''I would be terribly disappointed in you if you didn't,'' whispered Charlie.

Marita settled back in her seat and smiled to herself, as though thinking about the results of their conspiracy. Turning once more, she said, ''I hope you know that you are loved by more people than those in the LPGA and your father.''

Charlie's hand touched hers lightly. ''Thank you.''

''Yes,'' Marita continued, musing aloud, ''I know several people at Las Hadas who will miss you more than they are likely to admit.''

CHAPTER 9

DEAR DAD, IT FEELS GOOD to be on the road again doing my thing! I knew I couldn't come into the Lady Keystone Open after three weeks of mediocre practice and *win*, but I surprised everyone, including myself, by placing seventh. I am encouraged to say the least. Believe it or not, Diego's one morning of helpful coaching with my wedge helped me out of a sticky situation at least twice during the second round. Thank him for me.

Do you remember my one burning ambition every year during this event? I have now accomplished it, and all because of you. I figure I have not only enriched my "stew of life," but, unfortunately my calorie count for the rest of the month! Beth Daniel— the gal who won the 1980 World Champion of Women's Golf title by one stroke—and I talked a local tournament director into taking us on a trip through the famous Hershey chocolate factory after our last round. We figured we deserved a reward for placing in the money, and it is ridiculous to visit Hershey, Pennsylvania, every year and not take in their claim to fame. We loved the tour, especially seeing the clever ways they decorate the compound—the street lights are in the shape of chocolate kisses! I'm sending postcards and a big box of their yummies to Alejandro.

I'm sorry Cort was angry about my leaving without his knowledge. It wasn't my fault he chose to entertain Señorita Delgado half the night, and then helicopter off to Taxco the next morning before seeing any of us. I left a brief thank you note for him in his study. That will have to be sufficient.

Love and chocolate kisses, Charlie.

Dear Dad, Thanks a million for calling last night. As usual, you were very perceptive in knowing I would feel blue. Winning the Peter Jackson Classic was a shock and a half, and not being able to celebrate with you for the first time took a little bloom off the pleasure and excitement.

Some of the gals were talking about it at breakfast this morning, and Kathy Whitworth heard them, bless her heart. She has planned a celebration dinner tonight for a few of us who are traveling together. It won't be the same, but it's nice to know they care. Friends are not only pleasant to have, but necessary for living happily, aren't they?

Kathy is one of the dearest women on the tour, and deserves every honor she receives. I honestly hope she wins several more tournaments before she retires. She will then surpass Mickey Wright in the total number of tournaments won in her career and set a new women's record—Mickey won eighty-two! Kathy has already broken another record by becoming the first woman pro golfer to earn over one million dollars. Of course, several of us will soon catch up and surpass that because of inflation and today's larger purses for tournament wins. Whew!

I am keeping all the news clippings I can lay my

hands on for your collection. I'll send them in a packet after the next event. I'm pretty sure the Mexican papers near you have little, or no interest in me.

Next weekend is the Mary Kay Classic in Dallas. Remember how hot Jan Stevenson's putter was when she won in 1981? She made almost every putt that day, and became the first woman in golf history to break 200 for fifty-four holes. That score is firmly implanted across the front lobe of my brain, and I intend to daydream a lot about matching or beating Jan's record of eighteen under par of 198.

You know, I have won the U.S. Open, the LPGA Championship, and now, the Peter Jackson Classic in Montreal—three of our largest tournaments in one year. *That's never been done before! If* I were to win the World Champion of Women's Golf tournament in late August, I could possible consider it a Grand Slam sweep! Not even the PGA has had a player accomplish such a feat!

Stop laughing, Dad. I know it's crazy to even contemplate it, but I intend to try anyway. Every year, in some sport, an athlete breaks an old record, or accomplishes the impossible. I have as good an opportunity as anyone to win that championship. Keep your fingers crossed, and *pray for me*. I intend to practice on my chipping and putting until then, and work for birdies on every hole. My motto will be to *one putt* . . . isn't that what you taught me?

I'm delighted to hear how well your project is going. Of course, I understand it takes a long time to build the tees and greens. Really, Dad, ''grass doesn't grow in a day'' was a miserable attempt at humor! Lucky for you, your lodgings are so comfortable. It doesn't hurt to have a beautiful, charming and sympathetic hostess around to massage your aching shoulders at the end of the day.

So Cort was surprised about my teaching ability. I

must admit I had two above-average students, but Cort is perfectly welcome to give me all the credit. It's about time he learned that most women want more out of life than a house, a husband, and money for shopping trips. Marita has more to offer than being a lovely hostess for Cort, and a loving mother to Alejandro. She wants to continue to grow, and expanding her life's experiences to include even golf lessons should be encouraged. Cort should have taught her the sport years ago! I hope my rather pointed hint is well taken by you know who!

I miss all of *you*, too. Please give my best to Marita and Alejandro. Don't worry about me, Dad. I'm fine, really. I'm spending more time on my knees these days conferring with my heavenly Father. I'm also trying to spend more time *doing* His *will* than in merely sitting around *feeling* blessed or unblessed, guilty or not guilty, sinful or pious, helpless or doubtful, or self-assured and positive about everything. *Doing* means living, and giving, and loving. I know I'm human, and that makes me a sinner. I also know I'm forgiven, so the less time I spend worrying about how good, or how effective, or how perfect a Christian I am, the better. Feelings are too capricious. Finally, I have learned that important difference. The Lord didn't spend all His time on earth teaching His disciples how to *feel* like a believer . . . His life was a perfect example of how to *be* one.

Much love, Charlie.

Dear Dad, In spite of the five birdies, and a 32 on the front nine, I lost the Mary Kay Classic in Dallas to Donna Caponi by one stroke on the eighteenth. The Bent Tree Country Club doesn't have an easy golf course, and my downfall was a pond in front of the green. Donna put her approach shot across the pond onto the lip of the green within twelve feet of the hole. She made it in one spectacular putt. It took me two!

138

I have a week and a half to work on my difficult shots before traveling to Ohio for the World Championship event. Wish you were here to coach me . . . but the sign of an expert should be the ability to remember previous lessons and to be self-motivated. Right? Pray! I'm having some trouble with that last maxim.

The house seems empty without you. Mrs. Devlin has kept it neat as a pin in our absence, and Mr. Devlin has the yard looking like a park, albeit this is the desert.

Dean sends you his best. I'm having dinner with him tonight, for old time's sake, he says. I wrote to him while at Las Hadas, and I believe he understands there is no hope of a reconciliation. I'll find out soon enough. Hope I'm not doing the wrong thing in agreeing to dinner. I want to be his friend, but nothing more.

I received Marita's note of congratulations last week, and was glad to hear Alejandro enjoyed the candy. I'm also glad he is continuing with his golf lessons, and that you are finding the time to give them. Could it be you were influenced to do so because his mother has taken up the sport? You're right, it does give you a great deal of pleasure to teach others something you enjoy yourself. Now I understand why you've been happy as a teaching pro all these years. Perhaps I'll do the same in the future. The option is there for me.

It's hard to believe Cort is interested in my activities. He gave me the impression he found me a general nuisance during my brief stay at his villa. With me out of the way, he can devote full time to keeping Mercedes Delgado happy. She is more his type. Sorry to hear he's so temperamental and preoccupied lately, although to tell you the truth, that sounds "par for the course" to me. Sorry about that pun. I couldn't resist it.

You will be happy to learn I'm finally getting a handle on my temper. I owe it to God's intervention in my life. I have returned to my former Bible study, rising a half-hour earlier each day to spend quiet time in study and prayer. I remember your telling me that Mom used to do that. What an incredible difference it makes to begin each new day with a reminder of what it really means to love and be loved.

Love from me to you, always, Charlie.

Dearest Dad, I'm over the disappointment of not making a Grand Slam in one year. I knew it was unlikely in the first place . . . it hurts a bit to know I'll never get another chance, that's all. This sport is too difficult, the competition too keen, to ever anticipate winning all the major events a second time. At least I had the opportunity, and that's more than the others have had, and may ever have. I thank God with all my heart for allowing me the experience.

With my third place finish, however, I am definitely in the top position as money leader, and that, in combination with my six wins this year, including the top three tournaments, should help put me in the Hall of Fame.

Yes, I have been losing a little weight. Was it that noticeable in the news photos? I guess the tension got to me, and I couldn't eat those hearty breakfasts I usually consume with such relish. Perhaps the secret was in your home cooking. Some of the gals honestly believe staying on the slightly heavy side increases the strength in their arms, and gives them more power for long drives. I did notice my distance on a few long par fives was not as good as in the past.

Don't worry about me, though. Mrs. Devlin brought over a cherry pie yesterday, and I've been working on it ever since.

How about you though, Dad? It sounds to me like you're working far too hard. Can't you take off a couple hours during the hottest part of the afternoon? You're not as young as you used to be. Please leave the digging and physical stuff to the workmen. Your job is to oversee and guide the engineer, not to build the entire course singlehandedly!

I'm glad Alejandro liked the new baseball hats. I sent enough for him to hand out to his other pals, Sarita and Julio. Tell Marita I'm duly impressed with her progress on the short par three course there. A score of 33 is superb. Now, you need to teach her to use her woods, and then fly her to Acapulco to play on the Princess course.

No, I really can't take time to fly down for another visit, Dad. In September, I plan to play in three of the four tournaments. Thank Cort for saying I was welcome to come. I never expected such an invitation from him. You must know by now how much he discouraged my being there before. He's a strange man. He fills every second of his time with business . . . he is obviously a devoted brother and uncle . . . but he's so dictatorial and brusque, and difficult to know. There's no sense in our worrying about Cortez. He's probably a workaholic, and there's nothing anyone can do about it. Can't Marita get him to slow down? Maybe it's a good thing Mercedes had to leave for another film obligation. Of course, a man like Cort isn't bothered by a little set-back like that. A gander always finds another goose. Right? By the way, see to it you don't follow his example! You can't burn the candle at both ends.

My evening with Dean was not pleasant. He was upset—an understatement—with my decision to re-join the tour, and honestly believed I had quit because I wanted to marry him. Why can't he accept my decision and let it rest? Will you mention it, if you write to him, Dad? I really do hate to see him destroy his chances to find someone else by waiting around for me. I won't change my mind.

I thought Marita and Alejandro spent the winter months in California, at Cort's other home, because of school. What gives?

Love and kisses, and God bless, Charlie.

CHAPTER 10

CHARLIE THREW DOWN HER PEN and flexed her fingers. Writing letters was not on her list of favorite things to do. Although she couldn't deny the joy of receiving them, she would much prefer calling her father via the telephone, but ever in her thoughts was the concern that she just might hear Cort's voice on the other end of the line. In her present state of mind that would still be too unnerving. She missed Jim's voice, his laughter, his loving warmth and teasing, though. Hastily scrawled notes were no substitute for the accustomed hours of discussion and lighthearted banter they had shared for so many years. One tournament ran into another without him, and not even winning another of the last three, and placing within the top ten positions in the other two, brought her the degree of satisfaction she generally felt. Winning and achieving success were definitely enhanced when shared with someone who loved you.

Licking the glue on the flap of the envelope, she pressed it into place, wrote the address in her large, careless script, and put a stamp in the upper right-hand corner. She should be thankful Jim was happy and involved in a project which brought him such personal pride and satisfaction. She had no right to monopolize his time.

Tying a navy blue sweater around her shoulders, she snatched her purse from off the bed, and headed for the door.

If she stayed in the cracker box hotel room one more second, she would scream. The walls were pressing in on her, and the sameness of the decor to every other room in every other tournament city she visited was driving her crazy. She would mail the letter and take a long walk before retiring for the night. It was a cool fall evening in Oakland, and the fresh air would clear the cobwebs from her head.

If it weren't for Cortez Ruillon, she would fly to Manzanillo for a week after the final round of the tournament. She would enjoy a carefree visit with Jim while basking in the sun and reveling in the wide open, uncluttered spaciousness of Las Hadas. Such a visit was impossible, both now and forever, though. Her love for Cort had not subsided in the least over the past two months. Indeed, it had grown to such painful proportions, she had become a recluse, drawing the disapproval of her friends, and the ire of several LPGA officials who wanted her participation in every promotional banquet and news interview. She had no interest in food. Sleep often eluded her, and on other occasions became the panacea to a long dreary day of moodiness and boredom.

Charlie walked until she felt exhausted, stopping only to force down a hot dog purchased from a street vendor. It wasn't really a good idea to tire herself the evening before the final round of the Sarah Coventry Classic. On the other hand, if she could fall into bed and sleep without tossing and turning half the night— dreaming about Cort, always Cort—the enervation would be worthwhile.

Toward dawn, Charlie knew the evening's effort had failed once again. Slipping out of bed, she padded to the bathroom and dug in her travel bag for the bottle of aspirin. Taking two with a glass of water, she avoided looking at herself in the long mirror over the sink and vanity. She knew she looked terrible. Her eyes were dull and the dark circles under them would have to be covered with thick layers of make-up for the next day's play.

Keeping the lights off, Charlie curled up into the orange and brown upholstered chair near the bed. Resting her head against the high back, she pulled her knees up, hugging them to her chest. At first, she kept her eyes fixed on the ceiling, watching the altering lengths and patterns of light as they changed with the rising dawn. As her eyes grew tired, she allowed them to close.

Why wasn't God replacing her love for Cort with something else . . . or someone else? She had never prayed so hard and so long for something in her entire life. Perhaps her problem centered on not saying, "Thy will be done," and meaning it. She was too accustomed to doing things on her own.

You win, Lord. I've been stubborn for too long. I am yours to use as You will. I belong to You. This is Your world. Tell me what to do. With the silent uttering of her prayer of submission, a verse of Scripture spoke to her heart. *Seek ye first the kingdom of God, and his righteousness; and all these things shall be added unto you.*

The solution to part of her unhappiness evolved with such incredible clarity and speed that Charlie was certain God had waited for her final act of total surrender.

She was one-dimensional. Her professional status had brought—and continued to bring—financial independence, fame, recognition from her peers, pride of accomplishment, and innumerable other personal benefits . . . all earthly rewards; but playing pro golf was so intensely time-consuming, she had allowed other interests, including her faith, to suffer. Her father had been right in admonishing her to broaden her outlook and experience . . . she *hadn't* fully developed her potential as a human being in a world of other human beings. Her life was orderly, but selfish. She wasn't using even a modicum of her talent for the benefit of other people. She needed to restructure her priorities.

Action solved problems . . . not *reaction*. So, rather than becoming a recluse, moping around between tours, she would open a golf school for young girls and share her talent and acquired skills with a new generation of athletically-inclined contenders. It was so right she wondered why she had never thought of it before! She would charge minimal fees of those who could afford instruction, and nothing of talented girls without financial means! Most of all, she would let it be known she was only returning to God what was rightfully His . . . and her daily watchword would become, *Let your light so shine before men, that they may see your good works, and glorify your Father which is in heaven* .

At peace, once the decision had been made, Charlie crawled back into bed and waited for the call to come in from the hotel operator announcing wake-up. There was a renewed vigor in her preparations, and she arrived at the country club feeling on top of the world.

Going into the fourth and final round, Charlie knew her game would be special. She sank a four-foot birdie putt on the first hole, and narrowly missed making an eagle on the second when her ball rolled to within three inches of the hole. Filled with confidence, she surged ahead of Beth Daniel, her neck-in-neck competitor, by aiming her approach shots for the pin on each successive hole, rather than settling for any-

146

where on the green. Her strategy paid off, and the gallery roared its approval when she sank a dramatic 37-foot putt on the eighteenth hole to win the Sarah Coventry Classic with a final round of 67, and a record-breaking 10-under-par 278 total, for seventy-two holes. Pat Bradley had set the former record of 9 under par, 279 total, in 1981, when she won the twenty-ninth USGA Women's Open in La Grange, Illinois.

Charlie accepted the accolades for her achievement with an added sense of pride. Each honor she earned had greater meaning now, because it would give her proposed school a better likelihood of succeeding. Her students and their sponsors would have greater confidence in her ability to provide winning instructions.

After thanking the tournament directors one more time, and waving to the pleased gallery crowded around the eighteenth green, Charlie worked her way toward the press tent. Someone fell into step beside her, and assuming it was Beth, her tournament partner, she grumbled, "I'd almost be willing to hand over my winnings, if it meant I wouldn't have to face the press again. That one reporter insisted on turning around everything I said yesterday . . . making me sound like a . . ."

"If you point him out to me, I'll see to it that he takes up plumbing for a living."

There could be only one person with such a deep timbre to his voice, only one person whose every word—whose very presence—could make her heart beat a wild jungle tattoo like it was doing now.

"*Cortez*." Charlie froze, and not for the life of her could she make herself turn to face him.

"Hello, Charlie girl. Congratulations. That final putt was the most spectacular I've ever witnessed, bar none. If you play golf like that regularly, I can see why you're considered one of the all-time greats. The gallery of fans loved you."

147

"Thank you." She had to look at him now. There hadn't been even the slightest trace of mockery in his voice. The sight of him had its usual effect on her limbs. Every ounce of energy was drained out, like spaghetti water through a strainer. He was even more handsome than she remembered, and the hardness from his eyes was missing. It was replaced by something oddly disturbing . . . tenderness? Clearing her throat nervously, she found her voice again. "Why are you here, Cort?"

"Do you need to attend this press conference, Charlie?"

"Yes, I do. You know that. I won the tournament. They expect me to answer the usual questions about how it feels, how I did it, et cetera." Why had he avoided answering her question? "Is something wrong, Cort? Why are you here?"

Cort paused, and then his rugged features softened into a smile. "Why don't you wait with all those questions until after your interview, Charlie? We'll have more time to talk, and in a place a bit more private than the middle of a crowd. Come on, I'll go with you."

"Still giving orders, I see," she complained, but somehow it didn't matter. She walked by his side to the press tent, a bundle of nerves, but at the same time proud of her victory and glad he had seen her at her best.

Fifteen minutes later, they emerged from the press tent. Charlie followed Cort to the parking lot adjacent to the clubhouse. They sat in silence except for the few perfunctory words necessary when Cort asked directions, and she gave them.

"I'll give you thirty minutes before I come up, " Cort told her at the hotel.

"I'll be ready in twenty."

Ten minutes later, she stepped out of the shower, wrapped a towel around her clean, wet hair, and rubbed dry with a second one. In another five minutes she had dressed in a blue oxford cloth shirt and beige corduroys, and pulled on a pair of soft brown leather boots. She had applied a quick layer of mascara to her lashes, a stroke of blush to her cheeks, and mocha pink to her lips. When a light tap announced Cort's arrival at the door, she turned off her hair drier, ran a brush through her still damp curls, and let him in.

Instinctively she knew he had come on a serious mission. He must have seen the wild fear in her eyes, because he said, "Come here and sit down, Charlie."

"No, I'd rather stay where I am. Tell me, Cort. It's Dad, isn't it? Something has happened to him. Stop putting it off, and get it over with." Her voice rose on a note of panic. "He's not . . ."

"Take it easy, Charlie—he's not dead." Cort took a step toward her, and ran one hand over his hair. "Your father has had a heart attack."

"Oh, no. . . ." She choked and covered her mouth with both hands, not even caring that her eyes were swimming with tears. "When did it happen? How bad is it? Why didn't you call me?" Her voice became shrill and angry.

He watched her through narrowed eyes, but didn't come any closer. "It happened seven days ago. It was serious, but not immediately life-threatening. We didn't want to frighten you over the phone. Jim knew you had an excellent chance of winning today and asked that I wait until after the final round to tell you."

"I hate it when people make decisions for me. I'm not an adolescent." She wiped her eyes with the back of her hands. "You're not lying to me? You're not trying to make it easier?" She swallowed a gulp and caught her trembling bottom lip under her teeth.

"I'm not lying. I had him flown in my helicopter to the best medical center in Mexico City. The doctors there are excellent."

149

"Is he . . . is he still there?" Her voice faded into almost a whisper. She felt helpless and unbearably lonely.

"We flew him back to Las Hadas this morning with a registered nurse in attendance. She has had years of experience with heart patients."

"I've got to see him. He'll need me." The tears started again, and she turned away, burying her face in her hands.

"Charlie." Cort's strong hands were warm on her arms as he turned her toward him and held her carefully against his broad chest. He pushed a clean handkerchief into her hands, and encouraged her to cry. "Go ahead, darling. Let it all out. Don't hold it back. You'll feel better. It's a lousy blow to hear something like this without warning."

"I can't . . . lose him. I . . . I need him."

"Shh, don't even think about such a thing. Where's your faith?" Cort's arms tightened, and he pressed his lips into her damp hair, and against her forehead.

"I've missed him so . . . much." Her voice wavered and she trembled uncontrollably.

"Of course, you have." Cort's lips spoke gruffly against her skin, and she lifted her face a little from his chest, allowing them access to her wet eyelids. "And he's missed you." Cort pressed a kiss onto each closed lid and murmured softly, "We all have."

Charlie welcomed his comforting, needing the closeness of someone who understood her pain. "I've been so . . . lonely, so lost . . ." She turned her face upward to explain, and Cort's lips brushed against hers.

"Not any more, Charlie. I'm here now." His whisper-soft words against her lips ignited the spontaneous fire that always waited on pilot between them. When she didn't pull away, he crushed her pliant body against him and began a convincing trail of tantalizing kisses down the side of her face and along the line of her jaw.

"Oh, Cort," she said in a strangled voice, new tears squeezing out from under tightly closed lids, "I'm so glad you're here." She reached up to wrap her arms around his neck, and unconsciously sought his lips with her own. It seemed the most natural thing to do.

Cort needed no further encouragement. When he tasted the soft salty warmth of her trembling mouth, he kissed her with a hunger that had nothing at all to do with the comforting of a tortured soul.

Willingly, Charlie yielded, meeting his ardor with the same greed, the same need, with a desperation that frightened her. All the love she felt for him was evident in that kiss. Then, as quickly as it had flared, their passion subsided when both of them suddenly remembered the reason for Cort's visit. As Charlie's lips slipped away from his, Cort pressed her head against his shoulder and held it there until the residual shudders from her crying had completely dissipated.

Ashamed of her breakdown, and the intensity of her response to his embrace, Charlie welcomed the opportunity to stay hidden from his eyes. Knowing it might be the last time he held her, she memorized the feel of his body against hers, the strength of his arms enfolding her. How she loved him! Surely God must be responsible for allowing that love to grow. *Help, Lord! I've never felt so human.*

"My plane is waiting out at the airport, Charlie. Are you free to return with me to Las Hadas?" Cort spoke in a normal voice, and its steady, matter-of-fact tone helped restore her sense of reality.

"Yes," she answered, pushing herself away from him. "I'll have to, uh . . . I'll need to notify the LPGA officials, though. We're supposed to leave for England . . ." She rubbed her forehead impatiently with her fingers. "I don't know what to do. Our first European tour begins next week. I can't think straight."

"There's no problem, Charlie, I'll fly you down to

see Jim, and after you spend a couple days with him, you can fly on to London and meet the others there.''

She met his gaze reluctantly, knowing he could read how miserable and uncertain she was. She bore his scrutiny as long as possible before hooding her eyes against him. "I-I hope you won't misinterpret . . ."

"Please don't apologize for anything that happened between us now, Charlie. If anyone is at fault, I must take the blame. I took advantage of you in a profoundly vulnerable state. Why don't we forgive ourselves, chalk it up to the tension we've been under, and vow to forget it?"

Three hours later, Charlie walked off the plane in Manzanillo with Cortez at her side, and slid onto the back seat of the Mercedes sedan waiting for them. Cort was a wealthy man, accustomed to giving orders and having them followed to the letter. At times like this, she could appreciate it.

Keeping her eyes trained on the tropical panorama through the car windows, Charlie tried to ignore Cort's presence next to her. She should be praying for serenity and the strength to hold herself together when she saw her father.

Jim was too young to die, too young to be so ill. She would see to it that he did nothing to put further strain on his heart muscle. She would hire all the live-in help necessary to cook the right foods for him, to take care of his every need. She would quit the tour again, and stay home to oversee his convalescence.

I have no right to beg for favors, Lord, not when my faith is shaken so easily, so often. But I am weak, Lord, and you are strong, and you have told me repeatedly in your Word that if I ask anything of the Father in Your name, You will give it to me. I am selfishly asking for the life and health of my earthly father. I am pleading for his life. Give us more time together, Lord. Please. In Jesus' holy name I am praying for this favor, and thanking You in advance for hearing my cries of help.

"Take a long, deep breath, Charlie, and blow it out slowly. You're working yourself into a frenzy again. That's it. Several more times now." Cort's faintly husky voice came through to her subconscious, and she followed his directions mechanically; but, when his hand enclosed hers to still their nervous twitching, she brushed it aside intemperately.

"Sorry," he said, feeling her flinch at his touch. He moved toward his side of the car, putting more space between them.

Charlie wanted to reach out and pull him back. How could she vacillate so often between wanting his attentions, and not wanting them? Nothing she did these days seemed to make much sense.

The chauffeur drove the car up the long driveway to the front entrance of Cort's villa. It was early evening, but a full moon hovered overhead, emphasizing the Moorish domes and minarets, and reflecting its whiteness with the dazzling effect of daylight. It was so undeniably beautiful, Charlie stopped halfway up the wide marble stairway to gaze about her in awe.

"Welcome home, *querida*." Cort touched her elbow lightly and urged her up the stairs. Before his words had time to register, the front door flew open, and Alejandro ran down the steps to fling himself into her arms.

"Charlie! Oh, Charlie," he sobbed, burying his head against her chest, and clasping her tightly around the waist. "*Tio* Jim is so sick, Mama has cried and cried. They brought him home, but they won't let me see him. Will you let me, Charlie? Please?"

She hugged him to her, murmuring words of comfort and encouragement as Cort had to her. Then, holding his tear-stained face in her hands, she smiled down at him. "We want to do whatever is best for him, don't we, pal? We'll try to persuade the nurse

153

that a visit from you would be a big help. Can you be patient awhile longer?"

"Yes, I can." Alejandro sniffed and wiped his eyes with the back of his wrists. "I'm glad you're back, Charlie. I really missed you."

"Thank you, darling. I missed you, too." She gave him another hug and kissed his cheek.

Cort guided Charlie through the entrance hall to the west wing of the villa. "We've set up a bedroom-sitting room for your father on the main floor. We thought it would be easier for everyone to attend to his needs, and later, when he can get around better, he won't have to tackle the stairs."

Cort pushed open the door to a large room, softly lighted by a table lamp placed next to a hospital bed. The bed had been elevated into a half-sitting position, and Jim Summers lay against the pillows with his eyes shut. He looked sallow and drawn.

Charlie caught her audible gasp of dismay with shaking fingers pressed hard against her lips. Everything swam before her eyes, and near panic, she halted to suck in a ragged sob. Cort prodded her forward with a hand at the small of her back. "Go on in. I'll wait for you in my study."

Hearing Charlie's step, the nurse turned and smiled brightly, removing the pair of reading glasses perched on the bridge of her nose. "Welcome, Señorita Summers. I am Señora Olga Fuentes, hired by Señor Ruillon to watch over your father. He has been waiting for your arrival with some impatience, I'm afraid." She placed her book and glasses on the chair and came forward to shake hands. "He has dropped off to sleep, but we will awaken him."

"Oh, do you think we should?" Charlie caught at her arm as she turned to approach the bed.

"But of course, *señorita* . You are very dear to him, and he will not trust my good judgment in the future if I deny him a visit with you tonight." She gently shook

Jim's arm. "Señor Summers, your daughter has arrived."

Jim opened his lids slowly, and it took a few seconds for her words to register. Than, noticeably pleased, his eyes searched the room and found Charlie. "You came."

"Of course, I came," she retorted lightly. "I won today, didn't I? And what's the big idea stealing all the attention with this grandstand play?" She gestured at the bed and Nurse Fuentes.

"Stop your yapping, and give me a hug, honey girl. I've missed you like the dickens." Jim smiled wanly, and Charlie saw a shimmering of a few tears cloud his gray-blue eyes.

"Dad, oh, Dad!" she sobbed, throwing her arms around him. It was too difficult being brave when the person you loved most in the whole world had suffered such a scare.

"There, there, Charlie. You mustn't be so upset. I'm going to be all right." He smoothed her curls, and patted her shoulders. "You can't keep a good man down. Isn't that the saying?"

"If it weren't," replied Charlie, sniffling along with a tremulous half-smile, "you'd make it up."

"Why not? There's nothing to be gained by moping around, or by playing the game of 'maybe I should have done it this way or that way.' "

"Are you shaming me, Dad?" Charlie caught the tears on her cheeks with the back of her hand.

"I wouldn't do that, honey, but perhaps we should talk about it. My health has nothing at all to do with my work here at Las Hadas . . . or with your not being here with me. There was nothing you could have done to prevent my attack." Jim's voice weakened and he sighed wearily. "It comes from long-time neglect, harmful eating habits . . . lack of proper exercise . . . and, in great part, from heredity."

"Are you sure it wasn't caused from worrying so much about me?"

Jim patted her hand and paused to catch his breath. Charlie knew she should end their discussion, but allowed him to continue. "I drink far too much coffee and use too much salt . . . and you know how I love ice cream. And on the golf course . . . well, I've gotten pretty lazy. Rather than walk, I usually drive a golf cart."

"How bad was your . . . your attack, Dad? How long will it take you to recover? Will you stay here, or can we go home to Palm Springs?"

"I believe those questions are best answered by Señor Summers' doctor tomorrow, *señorita*. Perhaps we should wait until then, and let your father rest now." Señora Fuentes stopped the discussion with a firmness acquired from many years as a nurse. She waited for Charlie to kiss Jim one more time, but made it clear with her stern demeanor that she was in charge of the sick room, and expected her orders to be obeyed at once.

"Good night, Dad. Sleep well. I'll see you in the morning. I love you." Charlie swallowed the lump in her throat, but her voice quivered anyway.

"Good night, honey girl. Glad you're here. I love you, too. I'm glad you won today. I prayed you would." Jim's voice dropped weakly at the end, and when Charlie turned to wave at the door, he had already closed his eyes. Señora Fuentes, who was cranking down the bed, waved instead.

Charlie walked listlessly back down the hallway. She paused at the foot of the stairs and pressed her head against the hand holding onto the banister. She was overcome by the weight of her sadness, and, feeling her knees buckle under her, she sank onto the steps and buried her face in her arms.

"Charlie, what in blazes are you doing!" Cort's voice was a mixture of surprise and impatience.

"Go away and leave me alone." Charlie's petulant reply was muffled against her knees.

156

"I wish I could," Cort mumbled. "I wish to goodness I could." He leaned down, hooked one arm around her rib cage, the other under her knees, and scooped her up.

"What are you doing? Put me down this instant!"

"Be still, or I'll drop you! I'm taking you up to your room. You're so exhausted, you can barely hold your head up."

"I'm perfectly capable of taking care of myself, *and my father, too!*"

"I don't see any evidence of that. You've lost too much weight, you're all hollow-eyed, and as testy as an old spinster."

"When did you get your medical degree?"

"It doesn't take an expert to see you're not taking care of yourself. You're going to put your father back into the hospital if you don't change your ways." Cort had taken the stairs with ease, and proceeded down the hall with no sign of putting her down.

"Don't tell me how to get along with my own dad," she ordered, kicking her feet vigorously to free herself. "We've done well enough for twenty-six years without your help."

Cort kicked her bedroom door open with a foot and strode forward to deposit her on the bed. She lay back against the plump goose-down pillows, and stared up at him, defiance written on every line of her tired face.

There was a weariness visible in Cort's eyes. He tarried by the bed, his arms folded across his chest. "It isn't necessary to be so contrary to everything I suggest, Charlie. I may not always be right, but I usually mean well. My intentions are honorable."

"That's a laugh."

"I know you refer to my mistaken understanding of why you first came to Las Hadas. I overreacted because . . . well, that isn't important. I apologize now for my boorish behavior. Please forgive me."

Here was the apology she had predicted would

come with time. Where was the elation she should be feeling?

"Try to get a good night's sleep, Charlie. Things will look better in the morning. We can talk then. I'll send Rosa up to help you."

Cort seemed unperturbed by her silence, and to Charlie, that meant he didn't care if she forgave him, or not.

He left the room so quietly Charlie wasn't certain he had gone, and, filled with remorse over her inability to meet his request on an adult level, she continued to lie there, exhausted. The young Mexican maid came with a glass of milk, and left again at her bidding.

Hours later, Charlie awoke to find that someone had removed her boots and covered her with a quilt. Rising in the dark, she removed her outer garments and crawled lethargically between the smooth satin sheets of the mammoth bed. Somehow she had effectively blocked out every event bringing her to such extreme fatigue. She slept deeply, curled around her pillow in the fetal position.

CHAPTER 11

IT WAS TEN O'CLOCK BEFORE CHARLIE left her room to rush down the stairs. She had dressed hastily in a deep purple terry cloth pant suit, and her still slumberous eyes were the color of velvet pansies. She had tied her blond hair into a ponytail with a matching ribbon, and Marita smiled as she met her in the hallway outside her father's bedroom.

"You look like a teen-ager with your hair fixed like that, Charlie." She gave her a friendly hug, and Charlie knew it contained a message of empathy and understanding.

"I'm sorry I slept so late this morning. You should have sent someone to wake me. I hope you didn't wait too long before serving breakfast."

"There's no need to apologize, Charlie. Cort thought you needed to sleep until you woke up naturally. As for breakfast, I usually eat with Alejandro before he goes off to school these days. You must know by now we decided to stay here this year. There's an excellent private school in Manzanillo."

159

She was purposely avoiding mentioning why she had decided to stay.

"Alejandro will do well here, Marita." Charlie gestured toward the room she had vacated recently. "Do you think Dad is still awake? I'd like to see him again."

"Go right in, Charlie. Señora Fuentes has already bathed and shaved him. He's so happy you're here." Marita's eyes glistened with unshed tears, and she pulled out a handkerchief from the pocket of her ruby silk chemise to dab at them with total disregard for her make-up. "You've probably guessed by now that I love Jim with all my heart."

"Yes I have, Marita, and I'm also sure he returns your love. Everything will work out in due time. You'll have your time together."

"I wish I had more of your confidence, Charlie."

"I went through my period of doubt yesterday, but when it comes to Dad, I refuse to give up. He's one of God's most humble servants, and he's surely going to be rewarded with a little earthly happiness. I've interceded on his behalf, and the Lord is going to heal him. He *will* get well, Marita, that's all there is to it. We just have to believe that, don't we?"

Marita attempted a smile. "I'm glad you're back, Charlie. You'll do us all good. I've spent too much time feeling sorry for myself this week. I know in my heart that God never gives us more burdens to bear than we can handle. I'm praying constantly for a stronger belief in His healing powers, and for a strengthening of my faith, but at a time like this, my own selfishness rises like a mountain to block the way."

Charlie entered Jim's room thoughtfully. He was propped into a half reclining position again, and Nurse Fuentes was reading the morning paper to him. His eyes were closed, and he still appeared wan and unrested. Putting on a bright smile, Charlie chattered with feigned cheerfulness.

"Good morning, Dad. You look a little perkier in the light of day. Did you have a good night?" She cupped his face with her sun-tanned hands, and kissed him with a noisy smack. It was difficult pretending light-heartedness, when merely looking at him brought such sorrow. "Mmm, you still smell like shaving cream."

"Good morning, honey. You look like a flower. You're a . . ."

"Don't tell me. I'll say it for you. I'm a sight for sore eyes!" Charlie turned to the hovering nurse. "Each time I return from a golf tournament, he tells me the same thing. I still haven't determined if he does it on purpose, or whether his vocabulary is in a rut."

Señora Fuentes laughed. "Oh, I have found Señor Summers to be exceptionally erudite. Of course, we've only spent two days together, and perhaps I've formed my opinion on insufficient evidence."

"What is this, a feminist gathering, with me flat on my back and unable to defend myself properly? I never thought I'd see the day when you'd resort to such underhanded methods, Charlie. When I get well, I'm going to deliver that spanking you never received."

"Is that a promise, Dad?"

He grinned at her. "That's a promise, baby."

"Good. I'll look forward to it. Especially the part where you get well." Charlie pulled a chair to the side of the bed. "Tell me about the golf course, Dad. How far along are you? Are you pleased with the way the fairways lie? Are the greens going to challenge the best professional in the world?"

"I believe they will. The basic course is laid out. The engineer is working on the bunkers now, and we have two or three more small ponds to position. There are innumerable details to work out yet, though, and every day we change something. It can't all be put on

161

paper. I have to be out there seeing it firsthand." Jim turned to gaze out the window of his room, depression clouding his face.

Swallowing hard, Charlie elevated her chin. "That's not necessarily so, mister. A boss is supposed to delegate responsibility, not do it all himself. One good thing about a golf course . . . it isn't in any hurry to be built. You can take your old sweet time."

"Well, we'll see. I'm sure Cort would like to get it done as soon as possible. It's good for business in a resort like Las Hadas to have a regulation size golf course for guests. Not everyone swims or plays tennis, you know."

"Cort isn't hurting for business. From what I surmised on my last visit, this place is full all the time."

"That's beside the point. Cort will want to find someone else to finish the course for him."

"Has he said so?"

"No, but he hasn't had the opportunity yet. Who knows how long I'll be laid up. I may never get completely well."

"Now that's enough of that talk, Dad! It's beneath your dignity, and it undermines your wonderful faith to even think like a pessimist. You're young, and in excellent shape. This heart business is nothing you and a team of doctors can't lick. And I'm going to help you here. We've always had a partnership. You've helped me with my career, and now it's my turn to help with yours."

"I know you mean well, Charlie, but you need to return to the tour. Aren't you due in England next week?"

"I don't remember the schedule. It isn't important."

"What have you planned for today?" Jim asked, apparently abandoning the inquisition.

"Nothing much. I want to visit with you as often as

162

I'm allowed. I'd like to speak with your doctors, and take a peek at your golf course. Has anything been said about how long your recuperation will take, Dad?"

"No, the doctors have been vague. I haven't pressed them."

"Your father was in the hospital until yesterday, Señorita Summers. You mustn't be in a hurry," Nurse Fuentes scolded her gently.

"My reason for asking had nothing to do with the time element, really. I was only wondering if we should plan to fly back to Palm Springs, to our own home. We don't want to be a burden to the Ruillons," Charlie defended herself calmly, but her intentions were filled with anxiety. Did her father prefer staying near Marita and Alejandro? If so, how could she bear being near Cort every day and keep her sanity? She couldn't keep picking fights in order to hide her true feelings from him.

"I hadn't thought of that, Charlie. If you speak with the doctors today, you had better inquire about my being moved. If my convalescence is to be a lengthy one, or if I won't ever . . ."

Charlie covered Jim's mouth with her fingers. "No negative thoughts allowed, Dad. Get some more shut-eye before lunch. I'll come back later, and when I do, I want to see more of the old sparkle in those gorgeous eyes of yours. If I can get permission, I'm going to bring Alejandro with me. He's desperate to gain admission to this room and see for himself that you're all right. He adores you, Dad. We all do, so for goodness sake, eat, sleep, take your medicine, and follow Señora Fuentes' instructions to the letter. That's an order from me!"

Later, when Charlie had finished eating the plateful of fresh pineapple and still warm crusty rolls, washed down with strong black coffee, she took time only to refresh her lipstick from the tube tucked into a pocket, before setting out for Cort's study. During the course of her meal, an idea had formed in her mind, and she was determined to make it work.

Knocking on the closed door, she opened it without waiting for permission to enter. She needed to show strength and resolution.

Cort was seated behind a massive desk of highly polished mahogany, strewn with the over-sized drawing papers used by architects. He glanced up when she entered, startled by her abrupt entrance, and hastily rose to his feet.

His study was the only room she had seen in the villa which was not built of white marble and stucco. It was paneled in dark wood with floor-to-ceiling bookcases, and an enormous fireplace filled one corner. It was a man's hideaway—masculine to the last detail. "You're looking a little better this morning, Charlie. When I peeked in on you last evening, you were sleeping so soundly, I hated to wake you. Come have a seat here by my desk." He pointed to a comfortable blue leather chair.

"I came in here to discuss my father, Cort. I want to come to some agreement about his medical care and his continued work on the golf course. Have you spoken with his doctors about how long it will take him to recover from his illness?"

Cort leaned across the desk. His attention seemed to focus on the tip of a gold pen which he rolled playfully between his fingers. "Yes, I have. They're not ready to venture more than a guess at this point, Charlie. Right now they want Jim to get as much rest as possible until his heart regains strength. Then they want to perform a few more tests. Apparently Jim has a couple partially blocked coronary arteries. If they can't be opened through medication, or other simple procedures, his physicians feel he's a good candidate for open-heart surgery."

"S-surgery!" Charlie had difficulty pronouncing the word. She had convinced herself Jim would be back to normal in a few short weeks. This changed matters considerably. She blinked rapidly to clear her vision.

"A few years ago, it would have been a serious problem, but not any more," Cort explained. "Such enormous progress has been made in cardiology these days, people with blocked vessels can lead a completely normal life after they've been replaced. You mustn't fear the worst, Charlie."

"I see. W-when would this surgery take place—if he needs to have it?" Charlie coughed into her hand to clear her throat.

"Within the month, probably."

"So soon?" Thoroughly distraught, Charlie was unable to think clearly. She had to do something. "I'd appreciate your help in making arrangements to have Dad flown back to the States then, Cortez. Such a serious operation should be performed by surgeons recommended by our own physician."

"You can't assume that without looking into the feasibility of moving him such a great distance, Charlie. We can consult with your family doctor and get his opinion, of course. If he advises against a long move, we can always fly him here to assist the surgeons at the medical center in Mexico City. It's only one hour by air. Your physician can bring the finest heart surgeon in the world with him, if it will put you at ease."

Charlie chafed under the logic of his argument. "My father's health is *our* problem, Cort, not *yours*. We couldn't possibly intrude on your hospitality when his recovery might take weeks, or even months."

"What about his job with me?"

"It'll have to wait until he's well enough to resume the work without danger of a relapse. If this surgery you talk about is so effective, he should only be delayed a few months."

"I can't wait that long."

"What do you mean? You aren't thinking of having someone else take over?" Charlie's head snapped up, and she sought reassurance from Cort's face, but his expression was inscrutable, as usual.

"I don't see that I have a choice. I have a contract with the engineer and various other work crews. They have all their equipment here, and a schedule to keep."

"You can't dismiss Dad, Cort! He's your friend. Don't you have even one ounce of decency?" She was standing now, leaning over his desk, her full pink lips curled in derision, her breath coming in audible pants.

"This isn't the time for sentimental decisions, Charlie. Jim's a dear friend, and I'd do almost anything for him, but business is business. I can't put a crew of fifty men on hold for some indefinite length of time." Cort leaned back in his chair, and watched her through narrowed eyes.

"I refuse to let you hand over Dad's golf course to some other architect! It means too much to him."

"Do you have another suggestion?"

"Yes." Charlie's chest heaved from the strength of her emotional involvement. "*I'm* going to take over until he's well."

"*You!* What makes you think you're qualified?"

"I'm Jim Summers' daughter, a professional golfer of widely proclaimed expertise. I've played the best courses in the United States, and know what makes them good ones. I'll consult with Dad daily, and direct the work as he indicates. I'll show him pictures of every angle of every green, bunker, and fairway, until he's up on his feet, and then drive him around in the Land Rover as soon as the doctors give permission. I know I can do the work, Cort. It'll help Dad in his recovery to know his job is waiting for him, to know he can talk about it, and take an active role in its completion when he has dreamed about it for so long. You can't take it away from him, Cort." Charlie's voice faded on almost a sob, and she waited to hear his reaction to her proposal in silent suffering.

"What about your European tour?"

"I won't go this year."

"What about your goal to make the Hall of Fame?"

"Do you think I'd put that before helping my own father? What kind of person do you think I am?" Charlie was shouting at him again, her violet eyes shooting live sparks, her face flushing with both impatience and frustration.

Cort extracted a folder from a drawer in his desk, and paged through the material with exacting, painfully slow motions. Charlie tapped her foot on the woven Mexican rug, and gritted her teeth. The man was so dastardly exasperating! He knew she was in his debt, at his mercy, and relished the power he had over her. How could she love such a man!

"Well, it's an interesting idea. I don't know how well the men would take directions from you. This is Mexico. Men here aren't accustomed to taking orders from a female . . . especially one as . . . as young as you."

"That won't be a problem, I promise. They'll know the real directions come from Dad. They'll cooperate."

Minutes ticked away. "All right. We'll give it a trial run, but I don't want Jim to hear about any of the problems, only routine matters needing his direction. If you run into any difficulties, I want you to bring them to me. Is that clear?"

Charlie could feel the color in her face, and she turned away from the lazy smile in his eyes. "Thank you, Cort," she said. "You won't regret your decision. The Las Hadas golf course is going to be one of the world's finest. You'll see."

"I'll settle for nothing less, Charlie. Now, let's go

introduce you as the new boss. First, we'll stop by Jim's room to tell him the news.''

For the next three weeks, Charlie's days fell into a pattern of sameness. She arose at the crack of dawn, dressed in shorts, a T-shirt, and sneakers, ate a quick breakfast and hurried out to play a round of golf on the par-3 course.

After the round, she drove a cart about the new course, pinpointing the work her father wanted accomplished that day. By the time the workers arrived at eight o'clock, she was ready to give them their directions with the knowledge she was in charge, and could be trusted to be accurate, firm, and fair. She worked closely with the engineer who soon came to admire her attention to detail. With the trained eye of a golfer, she was able to see the rise and fall of the terrain, the width of the fairways, the position of bunkers, trees, streams and ponds, and the size and shape of the greens.

Every noon she returned to the clubhouse and gave lessons to Marita and a few of her women friends who had expressed an interest in bettering their game. She came to look forward to that hour, and as their skills improved, she not only shared their joy, but felt the pride of a successful teacher.

After a quick sandwich, sometimes eaten with the women at the club lunch bar, she returned to inspect the work being done on the course. When the men finished for the day, she took her Polaroid camera in hand and snapped pictures of each improvement over the previous day's activity.

A soaking in a tub of hot water liberally laced with bath salts, or a long shower and shampoo ended each day, before she dressed carefully to spend the time before dinner going over all the data with Jim. Together, they would compare his concept and drawings of a particular fairway or green with the actual

168

photographs. If any changes were indicated, Charlie would make meticulous notes. It was an amazingly efficient method of keeping Jim actively involved, and both of them found the project, and the collaboration, a gratifying experience.

Charlie's relationship with Cort changed as well. Daily consultations with him in his study, or at the table in the presence of Marita and Alejandro, brought a normalcy to it. She found she could participate in a variety of conversations without baiting him, or picking arguments in order to protect her delicate ego against his compelling personality. Silences were no longer uncomfortable, and on some occasions she shared moments of deep feeling . . . even laughter.

Three weeks after Charlie returned to Las Hadas, Jim was flown by helicopter to Mexico City for open-heart surgery. A widely known heart surgeon from Houston had already arrived to take charge of the intricate procedure, with the assistance of the hospital's surgical team.

The doctor's repeated assurances that Jim would come through the operation caused Charlie less anxiety than she would normally have experienced, though she could not help remembering in vivid detail the day two policemen brought the news of her mother and brother's deaths. Theirs had been such a closely knit family, and the unexpected and permanent absence of two of its members left a gaping hole that had never been filled.

They had cried to God for comfort, of course, and He had had provided it in abundance . . . but it had taken such a long, long time to accept. Her father's explanations of why her mother had died had always included the fact that everyone died eventually— some sooner, some later—and they would have to wait until God was ready to reveal the final answer to them. In the meantime, they would ask Him for enough strength to endure their pain, and they would remember that no one on earth is spared suffering—not even Jesus, who suffered patiently and selflessly for all mankind.

Charlie checked her watch for the third time in ten minutes. Walking again to the heavy door blocking the entrance to the surgery wing, she peered through the small window at the empty expanse of hall on the other side.

"There's nothing to be gained by all this pacing and waiting at the door, Charlie. Come and sit down." Cort spoke gently, and steered her back to the vinyl couch lining a pale green wall.

"Something has gone wrong, Cort. It's already an hour and a half past the time Dr. Bailey said he would be through."

"An hour isn't a long time when it comes to surgery. There might have been a delay at the beginning. Things can't always progress according to schedule. Dr. Bailey is one of the finest surgeons in the world, and he has performed this procedure thousands of times. Trust in his ability, Charlie, and trust in God to guide him. Be patient a while longer. Your father will be fine."

Cort took her hand and held it tightly in his. At first, she attempted to extract it, but the warmth of his flesh calmed her and seemed to refuel her rapidly diminishing storehouse of courage. His strength became her strength; his faith, hers. For it was very evident now that Cort had a faith to rival her own. Once, when she had walked over from Las Hadas to the chapel provided for its guests, she had found Cort sitting on the front pew, staring up at the ornate brass cross suspended over its altar. And, throughout their vigil, he had reminded her of God's ability to provide strength for their ordeal.

They sat without speaking for several minutes, and all the while, her mind was racing over the increasing importance of Cort in her life. If her father died, there

170

would be no reason for her to stay at Las Hadas. She would have to return to Palm Springs, to the LPGA tour, to her own life—a life without Cortez Ruillon.

"What's the matter, Charlie?" Cort's softly whispered question was as caressingly smooth as the stroking of his hand on hers. "Still worried?"

She could only shake her head mutely, and pull away from him. It would never do to tell him she was as much afraid of losing him as she was her father. Why couldn't she control her emotions off the golf course, as well as she could on it?

Rising to her feet, she hid her trembling helplessness with energetic pacing, refusing to even look at Cort or to acknowledge his repeated question. Several more hasty examinations of her watch only reinforced her conviction that Jim would never live through surgery. She was alone in the world. God help her.

"Charlie, Dr. Bailey is here. Jim's in the recovery room of the intensive care unit."

"Wh-what?" Turning a face of pure misery, she mumbled, incoherently, "Dad, h-he's gone? H-he didn't make it?"

"We had to replace two more vessels than originally planned, Miss Summers, but that's no more than many other patients with his particular blockage problem. Sorry if we caused you additional stress out here. There was no easy way to get a message to you. Your father is doing as well as can be expected." Dr. Bailey stretched his arms and wiggled his shoulders to ease the ache brought on by hours of being hunched over the operating table.

"H-he's *alive?* Not dead? When can I see him?" Charlie's hands clenched his arm convulsively.

"Not for a while, Miss Summers. It will take him another hour or so to wake up, and the nurses will be busy for several more minutes getting him hooked up to the monitoring equipment. He'll be kept in the ICU for a day or two before being assigned a private room.

Why don't you go to your hotel and catch a nap, or have some dinner? We'll call you when he's ready."

"No, no, I couldn't do that. I'm not hungry. I'll wait here."

Cort drew Charlie into the protective custody of his arms. "Dr. Bailey is taking good care of him, Charlie. He wouldn't advise you to leave for a single minute, if he thought there were a chance Jim would need you here." He brushed his lips across the top of her forehead before addressing the patiently waiting physician. "We're deeply grateful to you for agreeing to fly down here, doctor. I gave you the phone number where my pilot can be reached. Any time you're ready to return to Houston, he'll be available."

"Thank you. I think I'll wait until tomorrow. I'd like to give Mr. Summers one full night and check him out in the morning before I leave."

"Whatever you decide is fine. My secretary will contact you in a few days about the rest of our business." Cort gave the portly physician a knowing look over Charlie's head.

Charlie was too distracted to think clearly about anything. Cort was taking charge, but for once she didn't mind. Was Dr. Bailey telling them the truth, or was he lying to protect her? Why wouldn't he let her see Jim?

An hour later, Cort opened the door to Charlie's hotel room and flicked on the switch lighting the bedside and vanity lamps. "Take a hot shower, and climb into bed for a while, Charlie," he said, drawing her into the room and placing her purse on the television set. "Your outlook will change once you're rested. I'll bet you haven't slept well all week, have you?"

"When I've seen Dad with my own eyes, and know he's all right, then I'll relax." She watched Cort move toward the door with uneasy eyes. "*Where are you*

172

going?'' She meant the question to be a casual inquiry, but her voice bordered on hysteria.

Cort's dark eyes softened with melting compassion. "I thought I'd go to my room down the hall and give Marita a call. I promised to let her know as soon as Jim was out of surgery."

"When will you be back? Where is your room? How will I know when we can see Dad? Will the hospital call you or me?" Charlie wrung her hands, unable to control the trembling taking over her entire body. Didn't Cort understand? She was in a strange city, in a foreign country. She knew little of the language, and couldn't communicate over the telephone. She was frightened about her father, afraid of being left alone, afraid of her thoughts, afraid of possibly having to face another death . . . what if they weren't telling her the truth!

Cort reclosed the door and turned. Charlie saw him approach with his arms open to receive her. She walked into his embrace eagerly, knowing he would stay to share her fears, help her face them.

She buried her head against his hard chest and clung to him. "Tell me again he didn't . . . d-die, Cort," she begged, her voice smothered in his sport coat.

"Jim didn't die, Charlie. He's going to be fine. I wouldn't lie to you about such an important thing."

When the slow, steady tears of sheer relief, happiness, and thankfulness to God began, Cort took her up into his arms and sat with her on the couch, rocking her as one would a frightened child. He held her until her unfounded fears had subsided, and until she lay limply at rest against his chest, emotionally depleted and physically exhausted.

Then, carrying her to the bed, he settled her against the pillows and covered her with the thin cotton sheet, then flicked off the light.

Weary to the marrow of her bones, Charlie allowed

her eyelids to flutter shut, and her body to relax against the soft support of the mattress. Through the haze of her fatigue, she heard Cort cross to the telephone and place his call to Marita. His words were once again positive, reassuring and believable. Lucky Marita, to have a brother who loved her with such infinite tenderness, who put her happiness above his own.

Suddenly Charlie heard muffled sounds, indefinable to her overwrought mind. She lifted her head to peer, terror-stricken, into the shadowy room. "C-Cort?" Her heart was pounding in her ears. "Cort!"

"I'm here." His voice came from across the room, comforting and deep. "Go to sleep now, Charlie. I'm not going to leave you."

Amazingly enough, she did sleep . . . peacefully and deeply, and when she awoke, Cort was sleeping in a chair near her bed.

She allowed herself the luxury of tracing his face with her eyes—every line and angle of it. She knew it by memory already—the heavy brows joined together prominently over deep-set ebony eyes . . . cheeks now roughened with the shadow of a dark beard . . . the finely chiseled lips sometimes tightened into thin strands of anger or cynicism, but more often full and sensuous and ready to stretch into a tipsy smile that never failed to snatch her breath away.

In his relaxed state, the dark forelock dropping over his forehead, he looked so sensitive—so achingly dear. All the tense moments were swept away in the fullness of her love for him and, before she could call them back, the words were out: "I love you, Cortez. Oh, how I love you!"

They were three simple words, spoken hundreds of times in reference to her father, and to her mother and grandparents when they were alive. But now, they took on new meaning. She had wanted to shout them from the mountaintops, or on the golf course in full hearing of the galleries, but they had remained her secret. Only in her dreams could the sacred words be uttered.

"I love you, Cort."

Instantly he was awake, training his eyes on her, and she gasped, conscious that her thoughts had taken form.

"Charlie . . . we need to talk." Cort's deep baritone voice was husky with emotion. He leaned forward, and the two black pupils of his eyes, enlarged to comprise almost the entire space usually occupied by coffee-brown irises, were mirrors reflecting the image of her own face—shocked, horrified.

"I . . . I was dreaming," she whispered, not really expecting him to believe her.

"We must talk, Charlie." He rose and walked to the window, opened the draperies, and peered down at the traffic congestion in the city streets below.

He had never looked as tall, as virile, as handsome as he did at this moment. Charlie filled her eyes with the sight of him. They were both quiet for several long seconds, and suddenly Cort spoke.

"I swore I'd never marry again after Helena died. I failed her in so many ways . . . maybe I've irrationally feared repeating my mistakes." He shook his head in self-reproach, falling into silence again.

His deep voice vibrated in Charlie's ears. What was he trying to say? She pulled herself to the edge of the bed and reached for her boots.

"In spite of my better judgment, Charlie," Cort continued, his voice husky with feeling, "I have fallen in love with you. There was nothing I could do about it." He turned to observe her reaction to his reluctant acknowledgment. Their eyes locked, and both of them could feel the magnetism that sparked immediately in unguarded moments.

"I-I didn't know . . . I-I never suspected." Charlie was incapable of moving. She sat in a ridiculous pose—one boot off, one boot on—and forbade herself to think beyond that very second of time. She couldn't breathe, but waited for Cort's next words.

"How could you, when I was purposely accusing you of being a devious, manipulative child, picking fights at every opportunity?"

"Cort, why?"

"Because my love was greedy and selfish. I wanted you for my wife, and I was too old for you. Your father was my good friend, and you were quite clearly young and visibly frightened of me. I didn't want to lose Jim's respect and friendship. So . . . I thought if I made you angry enough, you'd leave Las Hadas before it was too late. It was for your own good." He sighed deeply and turned a penitent face to her.

"I *was* angry. I *did* try to leave. . . ."

"Yes, you did. And when I realized how devastating those plans were to the others—Jim, Marita, even Alejandro—well, I just couldn't let you do that to them. To tell you the truth, Charlie," he ventured a smile, "your stubbornness and independence, your willingness to defend your stand made me feel so incredibly alive. . . that *I* wasn't ready to let you leave."

A spark of that fierce spirit ignited Charlie's quick temper. "*You* weren't ready! There you go again. Don't you think I have a mind of my own? Don't you think I should be allowed to decide for myself when and why and where I want to do something!"

Charlie was on her feet, pacing the floor of the small room in agitation.

"Of course you should, but you were leaving because of me. I forced your hand." Cort strode forward and captured both her hands in his, bringing them to his lips. His dark eyes shone with tenderness, and her temper abated as quickly as it had flashed. "I love you with all my heart, Charlie, and I want you to be my wife. Will you . . . "

176

"No, don't say anything more, Cort!" Charlie pulled her hands free and backed away. "I-I have to think about this clearly. You're going too fast for me." She sank heavily onto the couch and dried her perspiring hands against the rough nap of her corduroy pants. "I do love you, Cort. And even if we don't marry, there could never, ever be another man in my life.

"If you had shared your words of love for me several weeks ago, I would have thrown myself into your arms. Nothing in this world was more important to me. I was so smitten with you I couldn't eat or sleep. I had been totally disenchanted with my lifestyle. Playing professional golf, with the sole aim of winning tournaments, had gradually become meaningless. It seemed increasingly selfish and money-oriented.

"When I took a hiatus from the tours and came to Las Hadas with Dad, I turned to God for guidance in setting more worthy goals, Cort, and I rededicated my life to Him. Then one very special night, He finally revealed His plans for my talent. They mean so much to me, I can't abandon them to become just your wife. I'd never forgive myself."

Charlie paused to search for the exact words to express how thankful she was God had seen fit to bless her with a future which included not only her love for golf, but for Cort as well.

Experiencing profound joy, she lifted radiant eyes to Cort's gaze. For a moment, his penetrating look seemed to grasp hold of her entire consciousness, and then it withdrew, oddly devoid of expression. He moved with disturbingly casual steps to stand in front of her. He touched a finger to her chin and raised her glowing face.

"I understand, Charlie. From what I've observed of your talent and ambition these past few weeks, I know they're deserving goals, worth pursuing. You'll accomplish them and be an inspiration to women everywhere . . . a truly beautiful, generous, exceptionally loving spirit. You have my utmost respect and my heartfelt wishes for success and happiness."

Lowering his head, he brushed his lips over her forehead.

At that moment the telephone shrilled, penetrating the stillness of the room. Charlie stood suddenly, her face ashen. Cort sprang to answer it.

Looking up, he smiled reassuringly. "It's all right, Charlie. Your father's out from under the anesthetic and is sleeping naturally now. Perhaps we should go now. He'll want to see you when he awakens. We wouldn't want to miss the brief visiting time."

Charlie was both elated at the news and stunned into immobility by Cort's behavior. That was the end of the conversation? Cort had proposed to her, hadn't he? She hadn't imagined it? Pressing her lips together, she concentrated on a composed reply. "You're right, we certainly don't want that to happen." Expelling a heavy breath, she took up her purse, joined Cort in the hall, and waited while he checked the door to make sure it was locked.

Without further comment she took the key from his hand and trudged toward the elevators. With each step she was painfully conscious of his presence at her side.

Forgive me, Lord, but I simply cannot understand what has taken place these past few hours of my life. I have experienced the agonies of a personal hell, and then, from the depths of my fear about my father's survival, have risen halfway to heaven! I love Cort, Lord, and he loves me . . . so what happened? Why aren't we communicating again? If Cort is the mate You've chosen for me, give him another nudge . . . and make it soon!

CHAPTER 12

WHEN JIM SUMMERS WAS ASSIGNED a private hospital room, with assurances his recovery would be routine, Cort returned to Las Hadas. Charlie wasn't sorry to see him go. It had become increasingly difficult for them to fake even casual friendship in front of her father, or to carry on a basic conversation during the sharing of meals in the hospital cafeteria. She stayed at the hotel for the remainder of the week, until Jim finally suggested it was time she return to the supervision of their golf course.

During the next two weeks, she worked long arduous hours on the course, participating in much of the physical work better left to the men. In her spare time, she reinstated golf lessons for Marita and her grateful group of friends. After dinner, she spent every evening poring over her father's notes in the seclusion of her room. But, despite her concerted efforts to avoid contact with Cort, she found herself continually watching for a glimpse of him.

One weekend, Marita took Alejandro with her to Mexico City to spend time with Jim. Fearful of running into Cort while alone in the villa, Charlie lingered at the clubhouse chatting with Diego, rather than return to a solitary and silent lunch with him. Diego had become a good friend, and often played the short par-3 course with her in the early mornings.

She followed him into his office, with the idea of discussing her future plans with him. He had the know-how about the business end of operating a club. His advice would be valuable. When he excused himself to go for sandwiches at the snack bar, she wandered around the room, perusing the pictures on the wall and the trophies and other mementoes Diego had earned during his years as an amateur golfer.

A sheaf of architect's drawings on his desk caught her eye, and without hesitation, she began an interested study of them while seated in Diego's chair. They appeared to be plans for a new resort.

"I bought us ham and cheese on rye bread. Hope that suits you. I forgot to ask if you had a preference." Diego pushed aside the papers to make room for the tray containing their lunch.

"No, that's fine. I'll eat anything. Diego, what are these? I didn't know you did this sort of work."

He threw her a puzzled look. "I don't. Those are Cort's blueprints. I'm sure you've seen the originals. He asked me to take a look at the clubhouse design and offer some comments, that's all."

"Cort's plans? Is he building a new resort?"

"Very funny, Charlie. As if you didn't know." He took a large bite of his sandwich, and pulled a second chair close to the desk.

"No, Diego. I don't know anything about it. Where is all this going to take place?" Was Cort leaving? Perhaps it would be easier not to run the risk of seeing him on a daily basis.

"Honestly, sometimes you pretend to be so dense, Charlie. If I didn't know better, I'd think you were leading me on. These are the plans for your new facility in Palm Springs ... the Charlie Summers School For Women's Golf! You're designing the course, aren't you?'' Diego took another bite of his sandwich and washed it down with a long drink of cola. He shook his head before slanting her a puzzled look. ''You *didn't* know, did you? Have I let the cat out of the bag? Was this to be some kind of surprise?''

''I don't know. I-I don't know anything about it. When did you get these drawings, Diego? You must tell me.'' Faint stirrings of hope were turning flip-flops in her stomach.

''I don't remember exactly,'' Diego mused.

''Try! It's terribly important. I must know!'' Charlie begged, pulling on his arm. ''Was it recently?''

''No. It was before your father went to have his surgery. Cort was talking with me about your class— with his sister and her friends. He asked me a dozen questions about the activity. Did I think you held the class only for Marita's sake? Did it give you genuine pleasure? I told him I thought you'd probably teach the rest of your life. You didn't miss a single day, and seemed to look forward to it. You know how we always chat about such things. I wasn't wrong, was I, Charlie?''

''No, no, of course not. In fact, I had already thought I'd set up such a school some day, but I hadn't mentioned it to anyone, not even to my father.''

''Well, Cort must have extrasensory perception. He's been bragging to all of us around here about how talented you are, and how the entire world was going to know about it one day. I'm sorry I spoiled his little surprise. I would never have left these papers on my desk, if I had known. I have a big mouth.''

''You say Cort has purchased property in Palm Springs? He's had these plans for *me* to design the course and have a school there?'' Charlie had difficulty repeating the words aloud.

"That's right."

"Let me see them, Diego. Show me." Charlie shoved the papers toward her friend.

Diego put his paper cup of cola on a window ledge, shuffled through the papers, and stopped when the right one surfaced. "You can't have any more proof than this, Charlie."

Charlie read the title on the plans, drawn in bold square letters: THE CHARLIE SUMMERS SCHOOL OF WOMEN'S GOLF. In parentheses below the title, she read, (Course itself to be designed by C. Summers at later date.)

Tucking the plans under her arm, she kissed an astonished Diego on the cheek. "*Muchas gracias*, you adorable, wonderful man! I'll return these tomorrow."

Without asking permission, she ran to his Land Rover, parked outside the clubhouse, and drove off in a cloud of dust. Taking the cobblestone plazas at breakneck speed, she progressed through the arches, past the bungalows, and onward toward the villa, shining snow-white under the scorching midday sun.

All the while she drove, Charlie plotted how she would present this information to Cortez. Should she shower and change into something irresistible? Should she wait and confront him after dinner tonight? Should she break into his study immediately and demand an explanation? What did she want him to do about it? What was she hoping to accomplish?

Stupid questions, every one of them! She wanted an explanation because she had obviously misjudged him again, and totally misinterpreted his intentions when he proposed marriage. If he had *already* made these plans, *before* that evening in Mexico City, then Cortez Ruillon knew her, loved her, understood her like no one ever had before—not even her father!

Charlie slammed on the brakes of the land rover, turned off the ignition, gathered the drawings into her arms, and ran up the marble steps to the villa. By the time she reached the veranda, she was out of breath and out of courage.

What if Cort had changed his mind about her? What if he no longer loved her, if he no longer wanted to marry her? What if he had sold the Palm Springs property after feeling rejected by her?

Suddenly slowed by her uncertainty, Charlie blinked back the gathering of frustrated tears. She didn't deserve someone as generous and good as Cort. She was too head-strong, too pretentious, too indiscriminate.

Just as her hand touched the ornate brass knob, someone from the inside pulled open the heavy front door. "Charlie! What's the matter? Why did you come speeding up the driveway like that?" At a glance Cort took in her desolate expression, her violet eyes awash with the unspilled tears. "Did one of those workmen dare to . . ."

"No!" The quick denial trembled on her lips. "Actually, there is something wrong. Close that door and come in here, Cort. I want to talk to you!"

Without waiting to see whether he followed, she marched staunchly to his study, flinging open the door. The thin translucent paper containing the artist's drawings crackled prophetically in her arms, and she hugged them against her chest.

"What is this all about, Charlie?" Cort stormed into the room and slammed the heavy door behind him. He was in a vile temper, and his dark eyes denounced her behavior.

"I'll tell you what this is all about," she fumed, whirling at the first sound of his ire. "It's about *this!*" She shoved the drawings into his arms. "I *demand* to know what they are all about!"

"Why?" Cort's eyes had narrowed to thin slits.

"Why? You know very well *why!* They've got *my name* on them! They involve *me*, and you haven't said

183

one thing to me about it! Were you just going to write it off?'' Charlie was throwing her arms about, pacing the rug of Cort's study with long strides, and thumping her chest with a fist.

"Calm down."

"I'm not going to calm down until I get some answers, and don't think you're going to put me off, or walk out on me this time because I'll follow you wherever you go!"

"What can I say?" Cort walked around his desk and sat with such uninhibited ease, Charlie was provoked into continuing.

"Don't start acting like some all-knowing psychiatrist either, because you're going to be saying a lot before we leave this room! Did you, or did you not, draw up plans for a new resort in Palm Springs?"

"I did."

Charlie loomed over his desk and pointed to the papers he had carelessly tossed there. "Did you, or did you not, include plans for a . . . for a Charlie Summers School For Women's Golf?" Her voice had lost some of its vitality, but she finished the question without lowering her eyes.

"I did."

"Did you also plan for *me* to design the course?"

"I did."

Charlie had gotten this far, and had no inkling of what she should do next. Cort wasn't making it easy for her. Maybe he *had* changed his mind, and wanted to see her squirm. Maybe not. Maybe he was waiting to see what her intentions were. He had no right putting her through such torture.

"Well, you have some nerve, Cortez Ruillon! Why, in the name of all that's decent, haven't you consulted with me about it? *That's* what I was trying to tell you in Mexico City. *I* was planning to build a school. Right in the middle of your stupid proposal, you walk out on me! I was attempting in my own way to explain why I had to be *more* than a wife. I have to be myself, continue with my profession, and share my God-given abilities with other people . . . for His sake. All this time, you already understood that. You knew that's what I would want. Why didn't you listen? Why did you let me go? You . . . you turkey! I'm in love with you. I want to marry you. None of this other stuff will be as much fun without you to share it with me. Somehow I . . . I just *know* the Lord sent me here to Las Hadas to . . . to meet you!"

The tears were coming as fast and furiously as her words by now, and rolled into her mouth. She wiped them away with the back of a fist.

"Are you through?"

"No!" Charlie sniffed loudly. "I'm not leaving this room until I have answers, Cort."

"I can't give you any while you're ranting."

"Well, holler back! You usually do. I'm used to it by now."

Cort chuckled, amusement bringing all the fine lines around his dark eyes into play. He rose from his chair and skirted the desk blocking his access to Charlie. "Come here. I can't talk when you're parading back and forth like that." He caught her hand and pulled her reluctant body closer to his.

Her breathing deepened, and she felt the stirrings that only Cort could arouse. She averted her eyes from his face, and kept her hands fisted at her sides. If she touched him, she was in danger of losing control.

"You've had your say, Charlie. Now it's my turn." His voice was almost harsh, and she could feel his gaze on her face. "Charlie." Only her name, murmured by his lips against her hair, and she melted.

Why did they need words to persuade each other of their feelings, words to rationalize the propriety of their love, when a kiss expressed it so eloquently? If they spent more time kissing, there would be less time for doubts and anger.

"Charlie." Cort separated them grudgingly, his hands resting casually on her hips. His eyes caressed her, and she felt like a ball of putty. "As I told you in Mexico City, I fell in love with you on the steps of Las Hadas the first day you came. You knocked the socks off me, and I was unprepared for it. I was shocked by the raw hunger that nearly crippled me every time I looked at your beautifully honest face, and at the same time, I was chagrined by my lack of restraint. I couldn't shake the difference in our ages, in our experience. Even after I spoke of my love, and proposed marriage, I felt guilty. You have everything going for you in your career. I saw how much the fans love you. But after living without you in my house those few months, I knew I wanted you back permanently.

"Jim called me into his room the day you returned. He was concerned about your weight loss, and rather haunted look. He suggested you stay at Las Hadas and collaborate with him until he was able to finish the golf course himself. He wanted to keep his eye on you. I agreed without hesitation. I would have agreed to anything, but I told Jim I was in love with you. I owed him that, and the opportunity to change his mind and return to Palm Springs with you. That's when he told me he was convinced you were in love with me, too. That's why he had made the suggestion you work on the course . . . to give you time to make up your mind. With my friend's blessing, I set aside my misgivings, and proceeded to woo you very slowly. The physical attraction was there, but I wanted us to be friends and admirers as well. It takes all three for a solid marriage."

Cort paused, as though waiting for Charlie to protest her father's involvement. When she didn't, he continued.

"I had already bought the property in Palm Springs. Jim scouted it out for me last year. Golf is important

186

in that part of the United States, and I wanted to be a part of it. I didn't know at the time of purchase, that some day it might become a gift for someone so special to me."

Cort lightly stroked her upper arms, and Charlie grew restless. It was hard concentrating on words through a storm of emotions, but she understood enough to know Cort still hadn't spoken the ones she wanted to hear.

"I watched your work with Jim, and it seemed to bring you increasing enjoyment. I spoke to several of the workmen, and with Diego, on numerous occasions. They said you were genuinely enthusiastic about the work, meticulous about detail, and tireless in your pursuit of making the course not only a challenge, but beautiful as well.

"I conceived the idea of your designing your own course one day, of your becoming the first woman architect of a major golf facility. Palm Springs was your home, a perfect enticement. When Marita and her friends raved about your natural teaching ability, and Diego said you never missed a lesson, and spoke often of the pleasure teaching gave you, I thought of the school.

"By that time, I had told you of my love, Charlie, and you had returned my kisses with enough passion to persuade me you loved me, too. That's when I dared to hope you would agree we could be happily married, have a couple of great kids, and still continue with our personal interests, which are certainly compatible."

Cort stopped speaking, and the silence lengthened.

Charlie's eyes were still riveted on his face, but she was unable to read any sign of encouragement behind his lengthy explanation, or see any in his steady gaze. Unsatisfied with his answer, she grew uneasy. He had kept to the facts.

"Go on," she urged. "Everything you've said is in

187

the past tense, Cort. What about *now?* What about the *future?* Do you still love me? Do you still want to marry me?'' She grasped his shoulders and shook him. ''Tell me, right now! I can take it, and I have to know. I can't go on wondering, and . . . h-hoping . . .''

Cort shushed her emotional outburst the only way he knew how. When he unwound her arms from his neck and pushed her away, she felt weak and shaky and on the edge of tears. ''W-what did you do that for?'' she stammered.

''Because we haven't settled everything you wanted to discuss, Charlie.'' Cort moved to the other side of his desk, and opened a drawer. He fumbled inside and extracted a long envelope, throwing it onto the desk. ''Read this.''

''What is it?''

''Read it. It's self-explanatory.''

Charlie opened the envelope and took out a folded document. ''I can't read Spanish.''

''It's a marriage license made out in our names. I've had it for two weeks. I had no intention of letting you leave Las Hadas without becoming my wife first, Charlie. Marita left early today to give me time to be alone with you. We are to meet her and Jim in Mexico City for a double wedding, if you agree to it. Jim wanted to surprise you with his release from the hospital. It seems he is very eager to begin his new life with a new wife and son. What do you say now, darling? Have I answered all your questions? Will you marry me?''

Choking a little from surprise and a radiant happiness, Charlie nodded vigorously, covering her wobbly chin and trembling lips with her fingers. ''Yes,'' she whispered, ''yes, yes, yes.''

''You won't change your mind?''

''Never in a million years.''

''Good. I'll keep you to your word. Now, come

with me, darling. I have something to show you." He took her hand and pulled her after him.

"Where are you taking me?" She lengthened her stride to keep up with him as he led her down the hall, through the white marble entry, and up the wide curving stairs.

"In every Las Hadas, or fairyland, there is a secret room where a man can take his lady-love. I have seen you look up at mine with open curiosity on several occasions. I want you to see it now."

They entered a rounded tower and ascended the narrow, steep stairway. At the top it opened into a large white room made ethereally beautiful by a kaleidoscope of changing colors as the sun filtered through dozens of stained-glass windows.

"Oh, Cort, it's *unbelievably* lovely! It's like being in a chapel . . . almost holy." Charlie stood entranced, her hands pressed palm to palm, her fingers just touching her chin, as though in an attitude of prayer. Her eyes glistened with unshed tears, and she blinked them away. Did anyone ever deserve to be as happy as she was today?

"It has never been used, darling. I must have saved this room for us. Somehow, I knew in my heart you would find me." Cort gathered her into his arms and his kiss thanked her. "Charlie," he murmured, his lips near her ear, "let's begin our life together right now, in a way so special that we'll never forget it as long as we live."

"Your wish is my command," she whispered against his cheek.

"I love you so deeply, my life would never be complete without you in it. Each time I look at you, I know how full of joy Adam was when God gave him Eve." Cort lifted her face to his adoring gaze. "I'm waiting with eager anticipation for the moment I can make you truly mine and echo Adam's words. 'This *is* now bone of my bones, and flesh of my flesh.' But I feel you are already mine, Charlie, and our love is holy. I'd like to thank God for bringing you to me, and ask His blessing on our life together."

Charlie let the tears fall this time. All her secret wishes had been granted. God had laid his healing hand on her father and given him a new life to share with a wonderful Christian family. He had blessed her with a talent and purpose in life which could only bring continued rewards if she dedicated them for His use. He had authored a union with this dear, dear man, and together they would demonstrate the beauty of Christian love.

With Cort's arm encircling her waist, her hands enveloping his, she knelt beside him and offered her personal gratitude to God. Under a brilliant Mexican sun shining through myriad panes of glass, they entered a world far more fulfilling and serene, far more enchanting than the fanciful beauty of Las Hadas could have possibly foretold.

Later, while sharing the couch occupying one wall and enjoying the full effect of the sun's rays through the colored panes, they made plans and lived their future lives together in one short, dream-filled afternoon.

Suddenly Charlie turned to Cort with her eyes softly gleaming. "A moment ago, I was remembering the long list of problems I brought to God. First and foremost on the list was my temper. You must have been His answer to that prayer!"

Cort's eyes were laughing, and a tender smile tugged on the corner of his mouth. "I can't wait to hear the explanation for that preposterous declaration."

She slipped her arms around his neck. "You must have noticed by now what usually happens when I lose my temper with you," she said, finally meeting his gaze through a tantalizing fan of thick lashes. Her violet eyes deepened to purple and flashed a message of mischief, and her captivating smile widened. "Your talent for ending it is quite effective, but I think I could use another treatment."

Cort lowered his face to capture her lips with his. "Mmm, I'm going to enjoy these temper treatments, Charlie. I might even have to ask God to work a little slower for once!"

A Letter To Our Readers

Dear Reader:

Pioneering is an exhilarating experience, filled with opportunities for exploring new frontiers. The Zondervan Corporation is proud to be the first major publisher to launch a series of inspirational romances designed to inspire and uplift as well as to provide wholesome entertainment. In order that we might better contribute to your reading enjoyment, we would appreciate your taking a few minutes to respond to the following questions and return to:

> Anne Severance, Editor
> The Zondervan Publishing House
> 1415 Lake Drive, S.E.
> Grand Rapids, Michigan   49506

1. Did you enjoy reading HALFWAY TO HEAVEN?
   - ☐ Very much. I would like to see more books by this author!
   - ☐ Moderately
   - ☐ I would have enjoyed it more if _____

2. Where did you purchase this book? _____

3. What influenced your decision to purchase this book?
   - ☐ Cover
   - ☐ Title
   - ☐ Publicity
   - ☐ Back cover copy
   - ☐ Friends
   - ☐ Other _____

4. Please rate the following elements from 1 (poor) to 10 (superior).

☐ Heroine   ☐ Plot
☐ Hero   ☐ Inspirational theme
☐ Setting   ☐ Secondary characters

5. Which settings would you like to see in future Serenade Serenata Books?

_____ _____

_____ _____

6. What are some inspirational themes you would like to see treated in future books?

_____ _____

_____ _____

7. Would you be interested in reading other Serenade Serenata or Serenade Saga Books?

☐ Very interested
☐ Moderately interested
☐ Not interested

8. Please indicate your age range:

☐ Under 18   ☐ 25–34   ☐ 46–55
☐ 18–24   ☐ 35–45   ☐ Over 55

9. Would you be interested in a Serenade book club? If so, please give us your name and address:

Name _____

Occupation _____

Address _____

City _____ State _____ Zip _____

Serenade Serenata Books are inspirational romances in contemporary settings, designed to bring you a joyful, heart-lifting reading experience.

Serenade Serenata books available in your local bookstore:

   Watch for other books in both the *Serenade Serenata* (contemporary) series coming soon:

Serenade Saga Books are inspirational romances in historical settings, designed to bring you a joyful, heart-lifting reading experience.

Serenade Saga books available in your local bookstore:

Watch for other books in the *Serenade Saga* series coming soon: